Love Unscripted

Nantucket Romantic Comedies, Volume 2

Taryn Daniels

Published by TD Books, 2023.

Acknowledgements

LOTS OF LOVE AND LAUGHTER went into writing *Love Unscripted*, but there's more than the writing process that makes this a winning story.

A huge thank you to Gwen Cage, my fabulous editor. She helps everything flow smoothly and makes sure I don't get too cheesy with the comedy factor.

Love Unscripted was first released through Kickstarter. I have amazing backers who received an early copy which helped pay for the editing and cover design. I appreciate you!

The heroes that made this story possible are:

Katrina Williams
Ruthenia
Laura Lagace
Megan L
Christine D'Abo
Cherelle H
Nicole Valdez
Mary C
M. Kay
Kathryn Parson
Donna Lane
Naomi Craig
MF Caram
Lori P
Rosalie Pease
Lauren Roberts
Brett

Jennifer Jensen
Meg Fitzpatrick
Amy Knupp
Rochelle Sharpe
Alexandra Corrsin

YOU ARE AWESOME HUMANS! Your names will not be forgotten—forever in this book.

Thank you, Taryn Daniels

Chapter 1

Only someone desperate—we're talking, beyond-dignity-and-scraping-the-bottom-of-humiliation desperate—would participate in a reality TV show called "Bride at First Sight." You can count me out. Sure, arranged marriages work in some countries, but not in the United States.

I fiddle with my press pass as I crane my neck to get a better view. How can I get closer to the contestants and hear what they're whispering about? This isn't my usual gig. As a sports reporter for *MA Times*, I wear sneakers and sweatpants while I'm on the field interviewing players. Tonight, I'm all glammed up and smack dab in the middle of the grand spectacle opening night of "Bride at First Sight."

I smooth my hand over my satin cocktail dress. At least I'm not wearing a plunging neckline to get a man's attention. I want to blend in but not stand out too much—unlike some of these ladies' cleavage.

Sparkling lights surround me, making me think of the floating lanterns scene from Disney's *Tangled*. The dripping chandeliers could rival a Vegas casino. Everything about this glitzy ballroom screams extravagance. Nervous energy thickens the air as women in slinky dresses prance around like peacocks, vying for the attention of none other than Liam Ashley, the Thunderhawks' star basketball player.

I can't help but laugh at the absurdity of it all. Women who look like they raided Neiman Marcus on their way here are doing everything short of cartwheels to catch Liam's eye. The lengths some people go to for fifteen minutes of fame. I'm sure each contestant gets a wad of cash even if they don't get the groom.

As I take it all in, the undercurrent of tension between the ladies is tangible. The clink of glasses fills the room as the women nervously sip their champagne, their eyes darting around in search of Liam.

Cameras point at them from every angle, capturing every movement of this mad circus. And oh, the faces. The women are shooting poisoned darts at each other, all while trying to maintain their poise and charm. Laughter erupts like wedding confetti, but when Liam passes each standing table, they burst into jittery giggles and frantic fanning motions.

I remove my press tag and hide it in my purse lest I be seen for what I am—a snoopy news reporter. Weaving my way through the crowd, I attempt to catch snippets of conversation. *Anabelle. Jenna.* I read some of the name tags and lean in as close as I can without being obvious.

Jenna is rocking a sleek black cocktail dress that hugs her athletic curves. Her hair is styled in a gravity-defying updo that pulls so tight her cheeks are non-existent. "I heard Liam loves a woman who can shoot hoops. I've been practicing for two weeks, and I can't wait to show him my skills."

Next to her, Sarah's hair is arranged around a tiara, making her resemble Anne Hathaway from *The Princess Diaries*. "Did you see how he looked at me when I walked in? Talk about love at first sight. I've got this, ladies. I just know it."

I roll my eyes. *Maybe he was caught off guard by the ridiculous crown on your head, Sarah.*

I move to the next standing table. One too many drinks have a few women swaying. Lily has employed a cascade of hairpins to hold mounds of hair into tiny buns. She probably hoped to captivate Liam with her unique sense of style. To me, it smacks more of homage to Princess Leah's earmuffs, but you gotta give the poor woman credit for such a mammoth effort. I'm not sure what look she was going for. It could be in fashion, but I wouldn't know.

Lily gives a dramatic pout. "Ugh, I can't believe that bimbo over there wore the same dress as me. Who does she think she is, trying to steal my thunder?"

Tiffany, stuffed into a too-tight dress crafted from a thousand disco balls, flicks her hair over her shoulder. "I overheard Liam digs a woman with a sense of humor. Lucky for him, I've got enough jokes to fill a comedy club. I've memorized twenty one-liners and if I get a chance, I'll slip them into the conversation."

Twenty one-liners in one conversation? My eyes pop. I'm sure he will be impressed.

The opening lines of a new article percolates in my mind. I could use a sarcastic edge, something like, "Grab your popcorn and get ready for a wild ride of love, drama, and sequined cocktail dresses. Speculations will fly faster than a three-pointer in the reality TV world of 'Bride at First Sight.' Whom will Liam Ashley pick?"

No, that's cheesy. Excessive like Lily's hair mounds.

I want to dig deeper and discover the backstory of these ladies. I already know all I need about Liam Ashley. I once caught him taking advantage of an intoxicated woman at an after-game party... oh, what a schmuck. I'm glad I got to expose the truth. He acts like a hero, and teens admire him, but he's just like my pathetic ex-boyfriend. Once the fame fries their brains, they're all players. The off-court kind.

Liam mingles at each table, speed-dating. Sure, he looks amazing in his blue-tailored suit, and the effect is only magnified by his role as a potential groom, but he is far from husband material—ugh. I couldn't think of anyone worse. But this is all a game. A reality game. These women are in for the contestant's money and the spotlight. Do they seriously believe a marriage to Liam Ashely would last?

I would hate to be watched by cameras 24/7, knowing the world was analyzing every move, the disagreements, listening to every conversation. Yeah, no thank you. I'd rather stay behind the scenes and report from my writing desk.

The music fades, overhead lights brighten, and a microphone is tapped causing an instant hush in the room. The show's host, Martin Cortez, is about to make an announcement. I slink back to the edge of the ballroom, getting away from the blaring lights. Has Liam picked his bride already? He doesn't mess around.

LIAM

Finally. A slim man in a black suit raises a hand, and heads turn in his direction. I edge to the back of the room where I can relax without all these women staring at me.

"Ladies, on behalf of 'Bride at First Sight,' welcome to the most incredible night of your lives." The man has a smooth voice, the kind that commands attention.

And it gives me a break. The constant smile is wearing me down. I resist the urge to roll my eyes when the majority of the women glance my way. Several of them wink.

The one with the crazy buns all over her head seems about to stand up, but the woman beside her grabs her hand and yanks her down.

Why did my manager decide this was a good idea? He gave me some cockamamie story about it being good PR. Whatever. I want to help my team, but this is over the top. Marriage? Really? To a woman I've never met until tonight and know nothing about. What if she's an ax murderer?

"Liam is incredibly excited to talk to all of you. His decision will be made at midnight." The man at the microphone spreads his hands wide, his grin bright under the abundance of lights.

I'm used to playing under pressure, but not like this. Not when it involves women's hearts.

"Once Liam makes his decision, the fun begins." The man continues. I should know his name but I've met so many people tonight that the names have all muddled together in my head. I can't wait for this to be over. Though since I'm the only man on stage about to offer marriage to a complete stranger, there's no end in sight.

I should have asked my lawyers to get me out of this. My team thinks it's hilarious. It wouldn't surprise me if they're sitting around placing bets on who I'll pick.

Movement tugs at my peripheral. Alarm jolts through me as I recognize the woman standing behind one of the tables. She stands rigid, and a tight scowl pulls her mouth into a grimace. The reporter who wrote that slanderous article about me.

My hands curl into fists. I shove them into my pockets and roll my shoulders to ease the tension. I can do this. I can pick one of these women, marry her, and guard my heart for three months.

"You all endured an extensive interviewing process to ensure you are a match for tonight's bachelor."

Now I do roll my eyes. There are five ballrooms in the hotel, each containing a bachelor suffering through this same process tonight. Five impending marriages, each candidate understanding that we'll live as husband and wife for three months. Once the show ends, we decide whether to continue the marriage.

Trina the Twitchy Snitch locks her arms tight over her stomach and hugs her elbows. I find her scowl endearing. She's the only one here not trying to impress me.

Lindsay, one of the participants, stands and sashays my way. "Hey, handsome."

I remember her name only because it's the same as my cousin. I plaster on the smile I use for my promotional posters. Wait...where's the announcer? What's happening?

Lindsay bats her eyelashes and rests a hand on her hip. She juts one leg forward in a pose that accentuates her legs.

Heat creeps up my cheeks as she leans toward me, and there's a significant amount of skin exposed. "We could get out of here, right now." She touches my arm, then squeezes. "You could pick me up with those big strong arms and put this whole mess behind you."

"I appreciate the offer." I sidestep, and her hand falls away.

The other women stand. The announcement must be over, and I've missed most of it.

I'm doing this to help my team. The money will go toward my future and the sponsorships my team relies on. I remind myself of this over and over as more women crowd around me.

"If you'd all go back to your seats, we'll have a chance to speak again." The smile remains in place even as a sense of panic floods in and sends my heart racing.

It's why I'll never find love. These women are here for the money. It's the same issue I've always had when it comes to dating. I can never discern what's real from the act.

"Did you see our personality results?" Another woman elbows her way closer. "We were a ninety percent match."

"Oh, sure, Lily." Another rolls her eyes and purses her lips like she's about to go in for a kiss. "I'm sure you didn't google Liam and answer the questions based on what you thought you knew about him."

The woman cackles, and Lily flushes scarlet.

Why do they act like this? I understand the desire for a better life. What I don't get is cutting each other down and stepping on necks to get there. I'm not here to watch a cat fight. Could be the ticking clock that has these women acting out. I've seen Ferraris go from zero to a hundred in less than five seconds, but these ladies have dropped their manners at a speed that has my head spinning. Is this how they would treat me behind closed doors?

"Please, take your seats." I offer Lily my arm. "Would you sit with me?"

Trina's mouth pops open. There. Take that Miss Reporter. I smirk in her direction. The article she wrote is so far off the mark. But even today, it's the first thing my name brings up in a search list.

I'm about to spend three months of my life under scrutiny. Every moment recorded. TV cameras in every room of my house. My life turned upside down for entertainment. Playing basketball is where I excel. Not this. But it should offer vindication and prove I'm a good guy as my daily life blasts across TV screens.

Lily beams up at me, her hand gripping my arm so hard I'll have nail prints, as we saunter to the nearest table. I pull out her seat for her and then take my own.

"Tell me about yourself." I can't lead her off the cliff of hopes, but I have no intention of falling in love. Not after I broke my last girlfriend's heart when I chose my career over her. A fact that still pains me two years later.

Lily folds her hands in her lap and tips her head to the side. She's quite pretty. "I grew up in Maine, and I have a brother. Like you." She shifts in her seat. "Isn't your brother a doctor?"

"Pediatric surgeon." The pride in my voice rings loud and clear. I might be famous, but my brother saves lives. Lily's tight grip on my arm reminds me of his deeply competitive spirit. It's a good thing we're over the idea of competing with each other. Like when we were kids and he'd get mad when I beat him at sports. "What about your brother?"

She stutters an answer. "Oh, you know. He's in...um...broadcasting. Like news reports. He covers the games in Chicago."

I stand and hold out my hand. "Well, it was a pleasure talking to you, Lily." She extends hers and gives a limp shake, mouth opening and closing. I turn on my heel and walk away. I need air, but there's nowhere to go.

Trina stands in a cluster of women. She nods and smiles but doesn't talk to anyone.

Why? What is she really doing here?

A plan forms in the back of my mind. It's crazy enough it might work. Trina hates my guts. Her article made that obvious. What if I change her mind? If I can convince Trina I'm a good man and not the creep she's made me out to be, all this might be worth the aggravation.

I spend the rest of the night mingling among the women, asking their likes and dislikes. Most give me the same answers, which are the things they know I like. One offers to go shoot hoops with me, which would be a nice reprieve, but not happening.

The giant red clock counting down the hours finally hits zero. The host returns to the microphone. He drones on about how he appreciates our participation, then waves me forward.

Bright lights cook my head and shoulders, causing me to sweat.

"Liam, let's not keep these ladies in suspense. Who's the lucky bride-to-be?"

The grin I've worn all night tugs tight against my cheeks. Almost over. I make a show of scanning the room full of women. I head toward Lily, and she gives the women on either side of her a satisfied smirk. I turn at the last minute and hold out my hand to Trina. "I choose you."

Chapter 2

Heat scorches my cheeks as Liam aims his smug smile at me from his two-story height. He takes my hand and tries to tug me forward. My heels dig into the plush carpet. I'm not moving.

A cameraman swooshes around us, and the camera rises and falls.

Oh my goodness. This is a flipping nightmare. Wake up, Trina. This can't be real. *Not real. Not real. Not real.*

A chuckle rumbles from Liam's throat. He places his other hand on my elbow and drags me to the stage. Gasps and cheers come from either side of us, but the faces are a blur. Lights pierce my vision. I must look like a startled squirrel on a caffeine high, frozen into a meme-worthy pose. My legs are stiff, and my arms are wooden. Liam the Puppeteer snickers under his breath. He's doing this to get back at me. What a turd.

Imbecile.

Well, that's not happening.

If only I could get my jaw to work. I'm an introvert at heart. I love my quiet corner and always have my head in a book. This. This TV crapola is not my jam. I hate attention. I love journalism—but on paper, not in front of America.

Hypnotized by the camera lens, I imagine my sisters' bug-eyed expressions. Melanie. Pam. Are they seeing this? *Get me out of this mess!*

But the show isn't live yet. Or is it? I hope not. They have time to pick another lady. Start over.

The TV host greets me with a kiss to each cheek. "Congratulations." He twirls me to face the ballroom attendees. "Liam Ashley has selected his bride." He glances at the place where a name tag should be. "Tell us a little bit about yourself. Beginning with your name."

I grit out a smile. What should I do? How do I say this?

Liam wraps his arm around my waist and I stiffen. "She's a little on the shy side. It's what attracted me to Trina in the first place." He kisses my forehead. "Take a deep breath, you can do this. For us."

My neck snaps in his direction, and it takes every ounce of my self-control not to tear him to shreds in front of millions of Americans. No. He will not win. He will not make me look like a fool on national TV.

I manage to moisten my mouth and free my tongue enough to speak. "Are you sure you know what you're getting into? You're making a big mistake. I can get a little crazy at times." I let out a weird cackle, more than a little unhinged.

He chuckles too and swivels toward the host. "And she has the *best* sense of humor. I'm one hundred percent certain I've picked the right woman. The next three months will be marital bliss."

Martin Cortez laughs. "Settle down, Liam. We have several challenges coming your way." He directs his gaze to the camera. "We won't make it easy on the newlyweds. We will put their new love to the test to see if arranged marriages can still work in twenty-first century America. Each week, a new challenge will disrupt their lives. We'll throw in a few unexpected surprises when we need to shake things up a little. Tune in each week to see if Liam and Trina can stand the test of time. As of tomorrow, they'll have only seven days to organize their wedding. Will they survive their first week? Text your answer to the short code on the bottom of the screen, 1 for yes, 2 for no, or go to brideatfirstsight.com to make your vote."

As Martin finishes his statement, a wave of panic crashes over me. Wedding preparations? Arranged marriage? I stare at Liam, desperately searching for any sign that he's only joking and doesn't want this either, but he stands there with a confident smirk.

"Wedding preparations in seven days?" I choke out, my voice trembling. "There's been a mistake." I squint at the crowd and wriggle my finger. "Princess Leah. I mean, Lily. She'll make a better match for Liam."

Lily's head perks higher at the mention of her name.

Liam's smile falters, and he places his big hand on my arm. "Trina, we can make this work. Don't doubt yourself. We'll figure it out together."

Martin jumps in. "Ah, Trina, sometimes love finds us in the most unconventional ways. Open your heart and give this arranged marriage a shot. This could be the best decision you've ever made. Life changing, even."

I'm trapped, caught off guard by the pressure and millions of viewers watching my response. Alarm bells ring in my ears, and my thoughts race. How can I make my mouth move to get out of this?

The host's voice booms over the loudspeakers, "Well, America, it seems Trina is a little speechless. Let's give her some time to process everything. We'll check in with the couple tomorrow and see if she can find her voice and embrace this incredible opportunity. For now, they have a romantic evening ahead of them." Martin turns to Liam with a wink. "Your limousine awaits."

What the—? The show host winked. In front of my mom who's possibly watching. Like a tornado has caught me in its whirlwind, I'm swept through the crowd, hustled down corridors, and out into the brisk night air. My brain is fuzzy, but as soon as the door closes behind us, I turn to Liam and let him have it.

"What the heck, Liam Ashley!" I yell so loud, my lungs hurt. My voice bounces off the thick tinted windows of the mobile palace. "Did you orchestrate this whole charade to get back at me? Are you that petty?"

Liam's cocky facade cracks, his eyes revealing a hint of guilt as he fumbles for an answer. "Trina, please. Let me explain. I wanted to prove to you how there's much more to me than what you wrote in that scathing article."

I narrow my eyes, not buying his excuses. "Oh, so you knew I would report tonight and decided to take your revenge? Well, congratulations, buddy. You've managed to make a fool out of me on national TV."

He extends his hand toward me. "Trina, it wasn't just about revenge. I genuinely needed a chance to prove you wrong, to show you a different side of me. I hope at the end of the three months, you'll rewrite the article."

I scoff, pulling away from his touch. "Prove me wrong? By subjecting me to this ridiculous spectacle. Sorry, Liam, but your plan backfired."

My phone buzzes with a message, and I check the screen. It's my boss, Mike, asking about the progress of the show. Anger surges through me. Liam had colluded with the network to create this entire scenario.

"You manipulated all of this, didn't you? You and the network, trying to humiliate me for daring to write a truthful article." I glare at him, my voice shaking.

Is that remorse etched on his face? "Trina, I didn't—"

I hold up a hand. "I'm stuck in this mess. But I'm a woman of my word, I. Will. Not. Let. You. Win."

I dial my boss's number, my fingers trembling with the adrenaline pumping in my veins. "Mike, I've been set up, and I want out. Did you see the show?"

Mike sounds grave on the other end. "Trina, I had no idea this would happen. I'll see what I can do to rectify the situation. But if I can't fix it, we could make it work. This could be a great opportunity for all involved."

I nibble the inside of my cheek. Was Mike in cahoots with Liam and the show as well? "Call me back when you have answers. Thanks." I end the call.

As the limousine rolls on, I'm hit by a barrage of embarrassment, betrayal, and determination. Liam may have set the trap, but I refuse to let him dictate the course of the next three months.

With a deep breath, I turn to him. "You thought you could get away with this? Oh boy, you're in for a wild ride. You'll be marrying a reporter who will dig all sorts of nasty dirt on you. If I have to plan a wedding with you, you will hate every second of your existence."

I cross my arms over my chest and face the streetlamps as they zip by.

The limousine is deadly silent and then I hear it. It starts off as a tiny back-of-the-throat grunt, followed by a second one.

A snicker.

A chuckle.

A snort.

Full-blown laughter fills the cabin.

I snap my head to Liam. He's collapsed in the corner, red-faced, and cackling himself silly.

I grind my teeth. He may laugh now. Just wait. *Just you wait, Liam Ashley.*

Chapter 3

Basketball is my thing. I dribble the ball down the court, feint left around Cool—whose real name is Peter, but no one calls him that—and pop the ball straight through the net. Swish. I dance backward, tapping my fist to my teammates' as I pass.

Cool grabs the ball and heaves it all the way across the court. It clacks against the rim, spins all the way around, then drops in. He smirks at me and slaps high-fives around to anyone within reach.

"Yeah, that'd be *cool* if it was a legal shot." I hold up my hands and wipe pretend tears from my cheeks. "We're still up three points."

"You're asking for it, man." Cool follows me across the court as I jog backward. His grin stretches wider and wider. "Can't wait to see you married and living the sweet life." He elbows Tandy, another teammate. "How many practices you think he'll miss?"

"None." I spin around and grab the ball as John passes it my way. I race down the court with nothing but the sound of the ball drumming against the floor, and my own heartbeat filling my ears. This is what I needed. The loud squeak of sneakers and my teammates ribbing each other with every breath. I leap into the air and slam the ball through the hoop.

I hang suspended in midair, defying gravity and all the emotions that have threatened to drown me since the night I picked Trina as my future bride.

The look on her face in the limo. She was so adamant that she'd make my life miserable, I laughed until I leaked tears. I didn't have the heart to tell her this whole thing makes me sick to my stomach.

I release the hoop and drop, landing with a thud that rattles my legs. The rim bounces back with a clang.

Cool snags the ball and holds it on his hip.

The entire team groans.

As team captain, Cool gets the final say in most anything related to our game. Him stopping our practice like this means something big is coming down the pipe.

"We need your head in the game." Cool stares me down. "For real. I get this whole PR marriage, whatever you want to call it."

"Yeah, Liam." John scrubs a towel over his face and drops onto the bleachers.

We're practicing in our home court, the place where we play the majority of our games. I'll never forget the first time I stepped inside. A massive dome covers the court and bleachers. Old jerseys line the rafters. And the smell. I breathe it in and hold it close. There's nothing like the mixture of excitement, popcorn, and entertainment. And sweat. We could do without the sweat stench.

"What? I'm focused." I reach out to smack the ball from Cool's grip.

He pivots on his heel, grabs the ball in one massive hand, and holds it out to me. "Do I get to be in the wedding?"

I can't help my grin as a wild idea hits me full in the face. "Oh, yeah. You're all in the wedding. Can't get married on national TV without you." I pucker my lips at Cool. "You want to stand at the altar with me too?"

He snorts and passes the ball over my head. Not an easy feat. I jump, and my fingertips graze the ball enough to send it off course.

Tandy shouts and snatches the ball, and the race is on.

"Hey, Liam. Phone for you." Coach Bristol pokes his head from his office, holding out the corded landline. The only phone that's allowed in the gym during practice. All our cell phones are shut away in our lockers until Cool and Coach release us.

I grab a water bottle and towel as I leave the court.

Hoots and hollers follow me to Coach's door. I grab the receiver and listen while guzzling water and toweling my face.

A disembodied voice travels through the line. "Liam Ashley, you have an appointment in an hour with Trina Smith at Cakes To More. The address has been sent to your email."

"I'm at practice." I eye Coach, who shakes his head and goes back to scouring the pages of our playbook.

"The producers at 'Bride at First Sight' require you to join Trina today for wedding preparations." There's a beep, then, "Do not be late."

The line goes dead.

I hold out the phone and stare at it like it might turn into a snake and bite me. Wedding preparations? I told Trina to do whatever she wanted. That I didn't care. I don't. Getting married isn't high on my priority list. Letting her call the shots was supposed to help smooth the waters. I recall her snarky remark that she'd make our time together miserable. Did she have something to do with this?

"Guess you better get a move on." Coach motions for me to return the phone to its cradle. I bet half the people who watch us play have never seen a phone like this. It's practically an antique. I cringe to imagine how many ears have touched that phone over the years. How many mouths have breathed and spit all over it? Gross.

"And take a shower before you go. You smell like last week's laundry. Look like it too. Better have a decent set of clothes around here. Can't show up in wrinkled gym shorts and a t-shirt." Coach smacks his chewing gum.

"Maybe they should've thought of that before they called me in the middle of practice." I chug more water and towel my face again.

"This TV stuff is important. Not as important as what goes on out there." He points at the guys. They've started another game in the few minutes I've been gone. "But still important."

I nod and back out of the office.

"Best foot forward, Ashley!" Coach calls as I leave.

The team sniggers behind me. They love when Coach uses my last name, which eggs him on.

I head to the showers. Half an hour later, I'm dressed in the only clothes I brought—a clean t-shirt and basketball shorts—and on my way to Trina's misery-fest.

My teammates make catcalls, their voices falling over each other in their haste to get in a smart aleck remark.

"Cute shirt, Ashley." John bats his eyes and cups his hands under his chin. "Sure wish you'd picked me to be your TV bride."

Cool chases me across the gym and out into the parking lot while making kissing noises. Once the door closes behind us, he cuts me off and holds out a hand to stop me. "Look, man, it's all fun and games." His grin softens, and he slaps me on the back. "If you need us for anything, we'll be there. We stick together, even in all this."

"All this" being a wedding to a complete stranger that will be recorded and televised to the entire nation. We'll be followed around for three months as we navigate the waters of marriage and whatever "challenges" the producers throw at us.

I'd rather wrestle angry badgers than leave Trina hanging, even though she's desperate to make my life miserable. I won't give her any ammunition for another article.

I STROLL INTO THE BAKERY half an hour later. One whiff of the sugary confections and my stomach roars to life. I pat it while easing around the tables. Trina sits by herself at a round table in the middle of the room. She looks amazing in a business suit but her tapping foot ruins the calm façade.

People holding cameras stand at various points around the store. The cameras move from Trina to me and back to Trina as they work to take in the whole scene.

Trina eyes them every now and then, and her lips flatten into a thin line. It's too bad. Trina has a great smile, and this tension isn't giving her the chance to show off her true self. Wait. Where did that come from? Trina is the one who ruined my reputation with her inflammatory article. She *does* have a nice smile, though. Not that I'm going to let myself notice.

"You're late," Trina hisses from one side of her mouth. She angles her head away from the cameras. "They kept calling you."

I ease into the seat and nudge the fork and plate around on the table, glancing everywhere but at her. The bakery is an explosion of pink. Pink tables. Pink shelves. It's like a giant bottle of Pepto Bismol exploded in here. A grin breaks free. I smother it with one hand and clear my throat. "I was at practice. Didn't know I'd have to meet you."

She arches a brow and drums her fingertips on the table.

I start to reach over and take her hand. Nope. Need to stuff that need to comfort back where it belongs. I cannot afford for it to take over, even if I do want to impress Trina with my good nature. My stomach grumbles a protest.

A woman wearing a pink apron and carrying a pink cake stand heads our way. She beams a bright smile and sets the cake stand down with a flourish. "Before you taste, what's your first impression of the cake?"

"It's tiny," I blurt out. I pick up my fork and poke the delicate slice. "That's all we get?" Makes me wonder what they'd charge for a whole cake.

"Liam." Trina shakes her head, but a tiny flicker of amusement dances in her eyes. Her thin-lipped expression flees long enough to prove she's prettier than I remember. "It's a cake tasting. Our shelves contain the life-size versions."

I glance over my shoulder to where Trina indicates. Varying cake sizes crowd an entire wall.

A cameraman shifts his weight in my peripheral vision.

Trina's frown snaps back into place.

My annoyance combines with hunger, and I pull the tiny slice closer. With a swift and decisive stroke, I cut it in half and offer the larger sliver to Trina.

She cups her chin in her palm and starts to relax, only to straighten her spine and roll her shoulders back. Her gaze darts around the room as though searching for an escape.

"Here." I lift the fork toward her. "Tell me your first impression."

She takes the bite, watching me the whole time. Her eye contact is somehow sultry and does something to me, and I don't like the sudden softening in my gut.

I swallow my piece without bothering to chew. It's a bit bitter, and the crumbly texture is off-putting. It's grainy and rough.

Trina tips her head to the side. "Not bad. I'm not a fan of the lemon. Something a little sweeter?"

"I agree." I wipe my mouth with a napkin and settle the fork on the edge of my plate.

The baker gathers up the cake plate and rushes away.

I try to keep from watching Trina, but her constant movement fascinates me. She looks everywhere but at me, almost like she can't stand the sight of me.

"What's your favorite cake flavor?" I sip from my water glass and swish the liquid around to get rid of the grainy bits stuck between my teeth.

Trina crosses her legs, her casual slacks a contrast to my gym shorts and t-shirt. She tucks her hands into her lap, assessing me from head to toe with a cool expression. When she answers, her tone is polite and impersonal. "I'd do mini chocolate lava cakes. They're messy but delicious." Her shoulders curl forward as she sighs. "But since this wedding will be aired on national television, I'd choose something classy. A vanilla pound cake with raspberry truffle cream between the layers. A white frosting. No fondant. And a classy cake topper. Maybe something in gold or silver."

The baker returns. This time she has an assortment of plates carried by three assistants. They set the plates on the table. Tiny note cards indicate each cake's flavor and whether it can be used in a multi-tiered cake.

Trina selects one called "chocolate dream" and places it in front of me. "Tell me what you think of that." The challenge in her eye prompts me to eat the entire slice in one bite.

I roll it around and savor the explosion of flavor. "Not bad. Tastes like chocolate but with a delicate undertone." I scrape my tongue over my teeth. "It's almost fruity."

The baker claps. "It's strawberry."

Trina's eyes widen and she sits back in her chair. Her gaze shoots off to the left for the fourth time since I arrived.

I lean forward and pick another plate. I stand and move around the table, taking the chair next to her. "Here." I lift a bite of the cake between my thumb and forefinger. "Try this one."

The cameras zoom in on us.

Before Trina can react, I grin and mash the cake into her lips. "I need to practice this part."

Her eyes spark so brightly they gleam, but I can't tell if it's laughter or animosity burning there. She grabs a piece of her own and shoves it into my upper lip and nose.

The smell of cake overwhelms me even as I laugh and scrape it from my face. I plop the remnants onto an empty plate and let my laughter roll into great, big belly guffaws.

Off to the side, the cameramen and servers chuckle while covering their laughter behind their hands.

Trina's expression eases. She unleashes the full power of her smile and shakes her head. "You're terrible."

I grab my napkin and lean in close, trying to clean the cake from her mouth. "I like it when you laugh." I didn't mean to say it out loud, but now that I have, I wouldn't take it back even if I could.

Trina shifts away and takes the napkin from me. "Keep that up and you'll never see me smile again."

"Oh, are those your sassy pants?" I nudge her foot under the table. "You're spicy today."

"I'm spicy every day." She swipes the last of the icing away and folds the napkin into a perfect square.

A guy peeks around the camera across from me and motions at Trina as if encouraging her to do the same for me. But she won't. I don't mind. I had a chance to adjust to this whole charade. She's still figuring it out. I know better than to push her any more than I have already.

A woman clears her throat behind me. The baker stands with her hands clasped and her smile firmly in place. "Would you like to try a few other flavors?"

I pull my focus away from Trina. "Do you make lava cakes?"

"Liam." Trina grabs my hand, the move shocking me into silence.

The baker's brows pinch together. Her gaze bounces between us, then shifts to the multitude of cameras. "I can make that happen."

"Good." I stand and pull Trina to her feet. "We should get to the next venue."

My stomach gives another grumble of protest.

Trina's laughter reminds me of bubbles. "You should grab some food on the way." She hasn't released my hand, shocking us both. "Come with me. There's this great food truck a few blocks away."

"Now we're talking."

We step outside together. I sling my arm around her shoulders and tuck her against my side as the press of pedestrians crowds the sidewalk.

She stiffens, then angles her head and purses her lips. I recognize the expression. She's not sure about me. About any of this. I completely understand. I'd feel the same way in her place.

I wait for Trina to regain her composure and take off. Downtown traffic is ridiculous, and I keep my arm around her the whole time.

Tantalizing smells drift between the stench of car exhaust and hot asphalt. I take in a shallow breath.

Trina tucks a strand of hair behind her ear and steps out from under my arm. "Welcome to Charlie's."

A bright yellow food truck parked at the corner advertises a wide assortment of foods. Burgers and fries are at the top of the list, but toward the bottom, I see what makes my mouth water. Street tacos.

Within minutes, we both have tacos in hand. I call our driver, and we scarf down the food while waiting on him to pick us up.

"Don't you think this whole show and rigmarole is all a bit excessive?" Trina tosses her trash and brushes her hands together. Cars zoom along the street. Horns honk in a steady stream.

"Yeah." I agree without hesitation. "But it's what I agreed to do. My team is depending on me to make this work." I clamp my lips shut before more escapes. Remember who she is, Liam. She almost ruined you.

Chapter 4

I squeeze the hands of my sisters in the midst of wedding dress shop chaos. "Thank you for getting here quickly." I lean into Melanie's ear, mindful of the cameras around us, but I'm not mic'd today. "At least for this shoot, Liam doesn't have to be here."

Her smile is sympathetic. I've been texting Melanie—emotion-vomiting about this awkward situation, but on camera, I've got to wear my happy face.

Melanie pats my arm. "Adam and I wouldn't miss this for the world."

I squint at her. "You just like the five-star hotel."

Melanie laughs. "Guilty as charged. No complaints about that."

I'm thrilled that they're a great match. Adam is a true sweetheart. He dropped everything in Washington, canceled his physiotherapy appointments, and cleared his schedule to be with Melanie for the wedding next week.

The shop assistant hangs three more extravagant dresses in the fitting room. A cameraman scans the dresses from the hook to the bridal train. Under the lighting, everything is white and dazzling.

I take a deep breath, trying to push aside the whirlwind of emotions swirling within me. This whole wedding preparation feels like a twisted game, and I'm desperately searching for a way to navigate through it without losing myself in the process.

My sisters follow me into the massive fitting room. At last, a moment of privacy, but we can't talk loudly.

As I slip into the first dress, a mermaid-style gown with intricate lace detailing, Pam's eyes widen. "All hail Princess Trina."

I force a smile, admiring my reflection in the mirror. "Princess Leah should be here, not me."

Melanie frowns. "Who?"

"Never mind."

Pam steps forward. " Liam could turn out to be the prince charming you never knew you needed."

I scoff. "Let's not get ahead of ourselves." I lower my voice. "Not a real marriage, remember? It's all for show."

Pam wriggles her eyebrows. "You never know what could happen."

I shake my head. "No. This isn't some fairytale romance. Liam knows I can't stand him. It's nothing more than a charade. Anyhow, I adhere to the rule of past centuries. If the marriage isn't...you know, the deal sealed with more than a kiss, it's not a real marriage."

Pam and Melanie giggle but my deadpan expression sends them scrambling for composure.

"I won't get caught up in any fantasy," I tell them. Even though I'm kind of enjoying the planning phase. Liam will never know that. The initial ceremony is one thing. The marriage will be a whole different ball game.

As I'm reaching for the next dress, my phone buzzes. I speed read the text. It's from my boss, Mike.

I turn to Pam. "The network has agreed to increase my contestant bonuses." After the opening show, the producers panicked when they realized I wasn't part of the selection pool. Liam insisted on having me as his bride, leading to last-minute negotiations.

"And the newspaper promised a raise at work in return for exclusive reports."

Mischief colors Melanie's grin. "Well, look at you, Trina. Turning a fake marriage into a career opportunity. You're taking journalism to a whole new level."

I laugh, momentarily forgetting the TV crew on the other side of the fitting room door. Leave it to Melanie to find the silver lining in the most absurd situation. But I can make the best of this weird scenario. Watch me.

My sisters help me put on the second dress. The layers are never-ending, but between the three of us, we manage to work it out.

There's a gentle tap on the door. The retail assistant calls in a chirpy voice, "How are you doing in there? Ready to show us the first dress?"

Oh, that's right, I need to twirl around for the cameras. "Nearly."

I take a deep breath. I won't let this mock marriage define me. I'll stay true to myself, expose the truth, and navigate this rollercoaster ride with my head held high. All while wearing a glittery marshmallow.

I step out of the changing room. The retail attendant practically jumps, clasps her heart, and gushes recited praise about the gown. Is she serious or out for the big sale? I guess all the dresses have exorbitant prices as they don't have any price tags.

I make my way to a little stage set up in the center of the shop. With a flourish, the attendant places a veil on my head, as if it's the grandest crown in the entire bridal universe. I try not to giggle at the sight of myself in the mirror, a combination of princess and poodle. If this veil could talk, it might say, *you're in way over your head, Trina. Run now.*

But it's too late for running. I'm stuck in this bridal vortex, swirling down the toilet with cameras, sequins, and forced smiles.

"What do you think?" The woman asks.

I could go with this gown as a start to Liam's punishment for choosing me. Imagine his expression if I walked the aisle in this tulle balloon?

Priceless.

But I'll embarrass myself at the same time. I shake my head. "It's not me." I fluff out the tulle. "I'll try on the others."

Her smile remains in place. Not sure if it's from Botox. The way her brows are plucked in a high arch, she seems forever enthusiastic. "Of course," she says.

She removes the veil, and I wince as the comb catches on my hair. Neither one of us reacts. We're both pretending she didn't just pull several strands from my scalp.

I turn to step off the pedestal, and there's another cameraman kneeling before me. My heart leaps in my chest, and I almost trip on the train. My arms shoot up and flail in a backwards windmill. Pam is there in a flash and steadies my descent down the steps.

My cheeks flaming, I return to the first dress I tried on—the one that actually fit my athletic body. It's simple but elegant, timeless yet modern. Perfect for me in every way—except for the ridiculous veil they put on my head earlier.

Pam gets a text on her iPhone and her face lights up. "Aw. Dalton is so great."

"Let me see." Melanie squeezes in between us and peeks over Pam's shoulder. "Cute! Dalton's such a great stepdad to Rex."

I peer at the screen, and now we're all scrolling through the photos Dalton sent. They're at the zoo for the day, keeping little Rex out of trouble.

Melanie enlarges the one of her husband, Adam, and nephew Rex acting like monkeys in front of the Orangutan enclosure. "What a good uncle he is. And might I say, daddy material, right there."

Pam angles her head. "You're not pregnant, are you?"

"Not yet. We're open to it, though." Melanie's cheeks turn pink. "Let's just say, we aren't avoiding pregnancy. If it happens, it happens."

Pam wraps her arms around Melanie's neck. "So exciting. Rex will have a little cousin."

Melanie laughs.

I stand there watching my sisters' excitement over having families. When will my time come? Will it be years before I can add a cousin to the family? Will my sisters' children be teenagers by then?

I tried dating apps after my last boyfriend, but I've been single for a while and would still rather sing karaoke in front of millions than try a relationship again. I don't trust men right now. But I'm sure there are good ones out there somewhere. Adam and Dalton are proof.

Pam tucks her phone into her handbag. "Sorry, Trina. This day is about you." Her gaze travels over my dress. "I love that one."

"Behold, the chosen gown," I say to my sisters.

Melanie's eyes widen, and she seems taken aback by my decisiveness.

Smoothing my hand over the silk, I turn and step out of the change room to model for the shop assistant. "This is the dress."

There are murmurs of approval from everyone—including from those behind the pesky cameras hovering around us.

At the back of my mind, I see Liam smiling at me from the end of a church aisle. I blink that disturbing vision away. Who cares if he likes the dress or not? I'm doing this for me and my career. Instead of a wedding mud cake, he can eat dirt. His little plot is doomed to fail because he doesn't know how competitive I am. Sweet revenge will be served, and I'll be the one dishing it out.

Chapter 5

LIAM

I'm getting married today. I've been telling myself this all morning, but it still hasn't registered. I caught sight of the wedding cake earlier and nearly fell over in shock. I scoured the tables around the sugary tower and even called the bakery to confirm the lava cakes. She told me the producers canceled the cakes and chose the giant thing instead. Something about the show-stopping piece being a better fit than gooey chocolate.

Pity. I'd been looking forward to sharing a lava cake with Trina.

What is wrong with me? I'm not supposed to be enjoying this. It's an invasion into my personal life I never asked for. The crowd gawks at me, and I swear I feel judgy eyes.

I fiddle with my bowtie and stick a finger into my collar. "Why do they make these things so tight?" It felt fine an hour ago, but now I can't breathe.

My brother Clay rolls his eyes and smacks my hands away. "Leave it alone." He points toward Mom and Dad, sitting in the front row. "Smile at the parents."

I do as I'm told. They look pleased as punch. By the way they're grinning right back, you'd think I'd never won a state championship or brought home enough money to buy myself anything I could ever want. I grew up with nothing. Landing a spot on this team has been the golden carrot at the end of the stick. I've chased this dream from day one. Which is how they roped me into "Bride at First Sight." Ugh.

I stuff my emotions deep down where they won't affect my expression. This whole thing is a sham. I know it, Trina knows it. My parents act like I'm madly in love with the infuriating reporter. No way, no how.

"How are things at work?" I question my brother to distract myself from the cameras. I'm used to them, but not when the setting should be an intimate one. Trina did an amazing job. The place is beautiful. I try to take it all in, but my gaze bounces around faster than I can dribble a basketball down the court.

"I'm not talking about work on your wedding day." Clay harrumphs and straightens my tie. "Can't believe you're doing this."

"You and me both." I resist tugging on my collar again and glance down to make sure I haven't scuffed my shoes or gotten dirt on the tux. I could've rented the thing, but I bought it instead. Something about wearing a tux another man had worn—probably to his own wedding—didn't sit right with me. I'd make use of it. There are plenty of charity galas and other events the team's required to attend.

"There's still time to escape." Clay leans in close, merriment dancing in his expression. He holds my shoulders in a tight grip. "I'll hold them off."

"That's not necessary." My stomach heaves just imagining the humiliation Trina would face if I ran. Not to mention the looks—and extra practices—I'd get from Coach. So not worth it. I can handle being married to Trina for three months.

Clay folds his hands in front of him and moves to stand at my side. He clears his throat and looks at the pianist—a young man wearing a sleek gray suit sits behind a baby grand.

Music pumps out, the tempo too fast and enthusiastic for a wedding. Trina's idea, or did the producers override her choice on this too?

At the back of the room, several bridesmaids look around in confusion.

Cool sticks out an arm, easing one of the women to the side. He leans to whisper in her ear. She smiles and makes a shooing motion for him to go ahead.

What on Earth?

Behind Cool, Tandy and the others strike various poses. It takes me a second to realize they're from my promo shoot a few weeks ago. Cool lifts his chin. The music changes, the tempo picking up speed.

Tandy snaps his fingers and prances up the aisle.

Cool claps his hands overhead. "Come on, now. Everybody clap along." He shakes his rear, spins in a circle and motions for the next guy to move.

I cover my face with both hands as laughter spills out. I can't believe they're doing this to me. Wait, yes, I can. It's no worse than what I'd do to them if our roles were reversed.

Cool does a smooth moonwalk, sliding his feet all the way down the aisle until he comes to a stop by my side. He tips his hat at the crowd. Many of them whistle and cheer. The cameras pan the room, then zoom in on me and Cool. I slap him on the shoulder like I'd known about this all along.

"You're so dead." I lower my voice to a hiss the mics can't pick up.

Cool shrugs. "Nah, man. They loved it. Makes the team look good."

He isn't wrong. Except for one small detail.

Tandy is still out there. The man has zero rhythm. He's bebopping out of sync with the pulsing beat. People give him pitying looks. I push Cool in Tandy's direction. "Go save him from himself."

Cool grins and chases Tandy down, then drags him over to stand at the edge of the room.

I shake my head at them and mouth, "I'm going to get you for this."

Cool brushes his hands together in a *whatever* gesture and rocks onto his heels.

The others snap their fingers and spin in a circle, wiggling their fingers at the women who must be Trina's sisters. I'd done a bit of research on her since the article, so I knew a little about her and her family.

I tried not to pry, preferring she enlighten me herself rather than leaving me to read and make assumptions as she had. I reel that thought back in. I need to put all that behind us. Ah, who am I kidding? I picked Trina to prove myself to her.

I'm afraid it's a hopeless case, me and her, but I'm too far in to quit. Not like I'd walk out on my own wedding. I wouldn't do that to my real bride, and the cameras would make it so much worse. Plus my team is counting on me. On this. I keep that in mind as the music changes, this time sliding into the traditional wedding march I'd expected.

The pianist is still laughing but his playing doesn't suffer. I'm glad for that.

My heart pounds when I see Trina peek around the corner. From the looks she shoots my way, she's ready to string Cool and Tandy up by their toes for ruining her sisters' entrance.

Sweat dampens my palms. I'm ready for her. I shoot her my best smile and steady my hands. Time to change my life.

TRINA

Liam's team members wiggle their butts as they do their pathetic dance down the aisle. How dare they shove my bridesmaids aside and take over. Melanie and Pam are laughing and don't seem to mind, but I do. I plunk my hand on my hip and send a laser glare to Liam. He's laughing too like he's having the time of his life. He could've at least told me. These kinds of surprises aren't fun. I like order. Lists. Even my underwear and sock draws are color-coded.

But this. This butt-wiggling show on my flower-strewn carpet runner is not acceptable. Marriages are built on clear communication, are they not? Okay, sure. I haven't been as open as I could have been with Liam. In my defense, I hate his guts.

Liam offers me a shrug. I paste on a smile that says, *buddy, I'll get you back for this.*

Fine, I get how he wants publicity. The Thunderhawks' cool factor will soar through the roof after this. As fans lap up the footage and send it viral, their manager will be in press coverage heaven. A brilliant idea, really. It's just, as fake as this wedding is, it's mine. I planned it, and who knows if I'll ever experience being a real bride. This might be my one shot. And Liam and his team have turned it into their show—Wedding Crashers, The Athlete's Special.

I need to practice my emotional regulation techniques and get my head back into the game. Eyes on the prize. I'm gonna crush Liam's soul. Insert witchy cackle.

Okay, that was a little dark. I'm not mean. I'll find something else to crush while he sleeps. Oh, boy. Do I have to share a bed with him tonight? I hope the hotel knows to supply a foldout bed for Liam.

I shake off that scary thought. The point is, I won't let myself like the guy, nor admire how much he loves his teammates. His signature smile won't catch my eye, where the right side of his lips turns half an inch upward, and how it makes his eyes crinkle at the corners. Not the way his broad shoulders and muscled chest fill out a tux.

No way. I will not appreciate one thing about Liam Ashley.

I must focus on what I need. If his team makes money and gains sponsorship from this marriage sham, I should too. My time in the limelight can help advance my journalism career. For too long I've been stuck at the same newspaper, getting the story dregs. Nope. It changes here. But I need to keep my cool in front of the cameras. Remain in control. I can't show my surprise when Liam pulls these stunts on me. I should pull a few myself.

The upbeat music fades and live piano takes over. The bridesmaids shuffle back into line, and Pam stands in front as my Matron of Honor.

The back of her copper silk dress cascades to her ankles, revealing silver heels. Curls and loops of hair flow to her shoulders. No expense has been spared to make this wedding exceptional and memorable. All should go well from here.

Pam nudges little Rex in front of her to take the flower girl's arm.

"No!" he shouts. "Girl cooties."

My stomach drops to the floor. Not now. *Rex. No tantrums. Not here.*

Pam bends at the knees and whispers into Rex's ear. What is she saying? *I'll give you a hundred bucks, if you'll do what mommy asks.*

I'll pay the kid a hundred—five hundred. *Rex, move it, buddy.*

Whatever Pam said, it works. Rex loops his arm through the flower girl's. She grabs a fistful of petals from her basket and showers them over the aisle as they walk.

My heart returns to normal speed and my shoulders relax. It's okay. There's usually one thing that goes wrong at weddings. People understand that kids do these things. *Just laugh about it, Trina.* Everyone else seems amused. Especially Liam. His eyes lock with mine and he's grinning. Good grief. I've got to kiss the guy in a minute. How will that go? Will we bump noses? No doubt he's an expert at kissing as all players are. But I'm not letting my mouth linger on Liam's. No matter how soft his lips appear. I'll lean in, give a quick peck, and pull back. I can do it.

Pam glides to the music, gracefully leading for the bridesmaids. My dad sits on a chair near my position at the doors. He injured his knee last week while dancing during the commercial breaks for *Dancing with the Stars*. He wobbles to his feet and moves into position next to me, taking my arm. "Ready, sweetheart?"

"Yep." I squeeze his forearm. "Thanks for flying in. How's your knee?"

"It's fine." He pats my hand. "Of course, I'd be here. It's your wedding."

"Yeah." I bite back the temptation to specify that this is a fake marriage. Dad doesn't need my drama. I'll let him enjoy the day and bask in the fairy tale dream. Someone should.

Melanie is halfway down the aisle, and it's my turn next. I take steady breaths, holding and releasing them in even counts to calm my nerves. I still don't like all this attention.

Before I know it, Dad is tugging my arm and leading my steps. One step. Pause. Next foot, pause. I'm doing it. I'm getting married.

I swallow hard as I approach Liam. He's the perfect groom. Handsome, tall like a beaming lighthouse no one can miss, and staring at me like I'm the only woman in the room. He's doing that lip thing, where one corner lifts. Oh, it's frustrating how sexy the guy is. If only I could turn off my attraction to the man.

Dad places my hand in Liam's, leaving the two of us alone. *Daddy, help. Don't leave me here.*

Melanie nods, her eyes saying, *it'll be okay. You can do this.*

Pam's biting her bottom lip. She's the epitome of *You're a fool if you go through with this.*

Looking up at Liam chases all negative thoughts from my mind. He brushes the back of my hand, and his gaze seems to convey, *I'm with you all the way. I've got you.*

I manage a smile, relaxing a fraction. I don't know why, but my gaze fixates on Liam's like a lifeline. I hate to admit it, but I need him in this moment. He's like a tower of strength I can draw from. Positive and sure.

I don't hear much of the sermon. Something about the ring being an endless circle of love. Goes on forever, or some other pretty baloney. We signed a prenuptial agreement yesterday that proves from the outset we aren't planning on forever. I don't know why the lawyers bothered to put in the bit about the prenup dissolving after nine years of marriage. We won't last a day after three months.

A long-winded burp snaps my head toward the front row. Oh, Gran. Why did you drink soda before my wedding?

Sniggers trickle through the audience.

"Excuse me," Granny Smith croaks.

Liam offers her his winning grin. Oh, he's even charming to the oldies.

The minister clears his throat. "Can we have the rings?"

Rex bolts to his feet, waving a velvet box. "Me."

I giggle. He's adorable in his mini tuxedo. A million times more charming than Mr. Ashley, here.

Rex rushes from the front row and his shoe catches on a table.

The table that displays the wedding cake.

The enormous six-tiered cake wobbles at the top end. It shakes like a mini earthquake hit, and the cake shifts into the Leaning Tower of Pisa. The crowd lets out a collaborative breath.

Phew. Not too bad.

Just then, when I thought all was okay—the bride and groom topper falls over. Well, if that isn't symbolic, I don't know what is.

Liam laughs.

He laughs!

I stare at him in disbelief. It's our wedding, dude. Don't you care that every possible disaster is happening? My grandmother belched on national TV.

Laughter spills out from behind him. The best man is chuckling. Pam and Melanie join in. Sitting on the bridal side, my mother reddens, her cheeks puff out, then she loses it too.

My mom has the funniest laugh, and I don't hear it often. I call it the rubber-ducky laugh. It starts as a soft squeak but ends as a honk.

I clutch my belly, aware of a subtle vibration. A sliver of amusement expands in my abdomen. It spreads through me like a wave and transforms into a torrent of giggles and—oh no . . .

I snorted.

Like a pig.

On TV.

I burst out laughing. The dam has broken. It must be from all the tension I was holding and I needed a release.

Liam holds my arm, rubbing circles over my back. Can this be any more ridiculous? He's trying to calm me, but his effort only makes it worse. My knees are weak, I double over, my hair flopping to the floor. My shoulders shake. I haven't laughed like this for—forever. Since I was a kid. I gasp in breaths.

I need to pull it together. Cameras are rolling.

I flick my head up, and my hair and veil go flying back into position. My face must be cherry red. Liam's holding back a chuckle. We must compose ourselves and finish the show.

He wipes a tear from under my eye. "Ready?"

I chew on my upper lip and nod. "Yep. Sorry about that."

"It's fine. Thoroughly entertaining." He winks.

The minister removes the rings from the box Rex offers so innocently—like he didn't just cause an uproar.

We exchange vows and rings, then the minister steps back. He pauses for a second before announcing to Liam, "You now may kiss your bride."

Oh, yeah. About that. My eyes latch onto Liam, and my throat becomes tight.

Air. I need air.

Liam tugs me closer and cups the back of my neck. It's a sensitive spot, and shivers run down my spine. I tilt my head upward, focusing on his mouth coming for mine. Maybe if I close my eyes, it will be over with quicker. But instead, I watch in slow motion and so does he. His gaze is locked with mine, and then it happens. Like an electric current, Liam zaps me as our lips meet. I blink and pull back as I planned to. But Liam leans down again, and his other arm wraps firmly around my waist. Heat swirls around me, cocooning us like a cozy blanket on a winter's night. My mouth relaxes as his lips smooth over mine. I breathe in his yummy cologne and softly sigh when he finishes the kiss.

He's smiling at me, and my cheeks heat. I sighed and he heard.

Dang it.

Claps and cheers explode around the room as our guests stand. I turn toward them. Liam holds our joined hands high. We did it.

Oh, flipping heck. I'm Mrs. Liam Ashley.

Chapter 6

LIAM

I'm a married man. The words roll around in my head, taking up way too much space. Trina stands next to me in the hotel lobby. We made it to Nantucket. Our suitcases sit at our feet. I crane my head back to study the chandelier that hangs overhead. Crystal bobbers dangle from it and catch the light.

I tried not to gape when we first arrived, but I have never seen anything like this before. Not even when I'm on the road with the team. We don't stay in places like this. Dollar bills dance in front of my eyes. I can't fathom how much the show is paying for us to stay here for our honeymoon.

All thoughts come to a screeching halt.

Honeymoon. I suck air through my teeth and avoid meeting Trina's eyes.

She's a statue by my side. The last time I glanced at her, she wore a bedazzled expression and let out a low whistle.

A man wheeling a cart rolls toward us. "Checking in?"

"Yes." I snap out of my reverie and approached the desk. "Liam Ashley."

Trina clears her throat.

Sweat beads on my forehead despite the cold air pumping overhead. I tug at my collar, a plain Polo collar instead of the constricting tuxedo thing. Why am I still choking?

The man behind the desk cocks his head at us. His fingers fly over the keyboard. "Mr. and Mrs. Ashley." His eyebrows lower, then shoot upward.

Do I even want to know what he saw on the screen?

"If you'll follow Chris, he'll show you to your room." He holds out a pair of keycards. "Please enjoy your stay." Something in his voice rings false. As does the plastic smile that looks more like a grimace.

Chris—the man with the rolling cart stacks the last piece of luggage. "Right this way."

We follow him to a bank of elevators. I expect it to be crowded with the three of us plus the luggage, but there's plenty of room. Room Trina uses to her advantage.

She presses her back to the wall and folds her arms over her stomach.

"Your dress was beautiful." I attempt to ease her apparent discomfort. If anything, I've made it worse if her sudden blanching is any indication.

She shoots a look at Chris, then meets my gaze. "Thanks." She rubs her hands up and down the goosebumps on her arms.

I grab my jacket from the stack of luggage and swing it around her shoulders.

The doors whoosh open. Chris walks out ahead of us. Seconds later, a door clicks open and he motions us inside ahead of him. "Welcome to the honeymoon suite."

Trina groans and holds her stomach. "I think I might be sick."

She's not the only one. There's a sudden churning in my gut when our eyes meet or I think about the room we're supposed to share. I make the first move, brushing past Chris and stepping into the room. Holy mackerel. My grandfather's favorite phrase helps ground me, but I still stare like I've never seen anything like this place. Because I haven't. Opulent doesn't begin to describe the lush bedding or the thick carpet muffling my steps.

Trina follows me inside, her steps hesitant. She stops near the balcony doors and pulls back the curtains. Ocean fills the windows from side to side.

Trina's shoulders lift and lower in rapid breaths.

I want to comfort her. I reach for her shoulders at the same time she turns. Her elbow catches me in the stomach. My breath rushes out in a grunt.

She tosses her hair and starts grabbing her luggage from the floor where Chris left it. The man slipped out without another word and without my notice. I'd been too distracted by Trina. Not good. I shouldn't be this in tune with her. I shouldn't be this worried about her. None of that was in my plans.

The overhead lights flicker. I pause on my way toward the kitchen area. This place is almost ridiculously luxurious. There's a full bedroom, a full bath, a kitchen, dining area, balcony, and a living room bigger than my own back at home.

Trina glances up and frowns. "Bad wiring?"

"In a place this expensive?" The fine hairs on the back of my neck lift. I trek to the door and pull it open. Dead silence. "We must be the only people on this floor." I glance left, then right.

The lights flicker in the hallway, then go out. I draw an unsteady breath and wait for panic and chaos to spill out from the other suites. When nothing happens, I retreat to our room to find Trina.

The fire alarm blares. Trina and I both jump. The lights beat a steady rhythm. A red glow emanates from the alarm tucked high in the wall over the kitchen. Red and white lights strobe around the room as the siren continues to wail.

Trina claps her hands over her ears. "What do we do?"

"Let's go." I grab her elbow and steer her into the hallway. I rush toward the elevator and jab the button. A frustrated sound leaves my throat when I remember the elevators won't work. "Stairs."

"What?" Trina shouts over the alarm.

I point and head toward the white door at the end of the hallway. We're on the top floor. Seventeen flights of stairs stand between us and safety.

Trina rushes down the steps. The sound of our pounding feet is lost in the screeching bells and the pounding in my heart. She stumbles and almost falls.

I wrap an arm around her waist and pull her flush against my chest. She grips my arm, her nails digging in. Her ragged breaths puff against my forearm. She's panicking.

Heck, I'm panicking. One of us needs to keep their head.

I sweep her into my arms and take off. I'm taller, with longer legs. I can move fast enough for both of us.

If Trina protests, I don't hear it. The weight of her settles in my arms. She grabs onto my shoulder with one hand, the other resting over my heart where she grips my shirt in a tight fist.

We reach a landing and Trina wiggles in my hold.

Her cheeks are flushed and there's more than panic in her eyes. They're almost—almost—warm. "I can walk."

I see her mouth move but the alarm is too loud for me to hear her actual words. I tighten my grip and barrel down another flight. Trina isn't heavy, but it's still a workout. Running seventeen flights of stairs by myself would have me doubled over by the end.

When we reach the next landing, Trina kicks her feet back and forth so hard I can't keep hold of her. I lower her to the floor.

She takes my hand, kisses my cheek, and bolts. And she's fast.

I match her stride, and we come to the end of the stairs, bursting out into the lobby. A dozen people look our way. The man who checked us in waves us over. "I'm terribly sorry. The firemen are here, along with the fire marshal. They will assess the building, but for now we must move all residents to other lodging." He holds out a packet. "The Rose Resort will be a great place for the two of you. Your luggage will be there shortly."

With those words, he spins on his heel and rushes away.

A protest builds behind my lips. I hold the brochure in the air, ready to call him back and demand an explanation.

"Oh, cute." Trina grabs the paper from me and gasps. "Oh my goodness. It's the same place Melanie told me about." She clasps her hands under her chin and beams. "I want to go."

And just like that, my decision is made.

"Mr. and Mrs. Ashley?" The man who drove us from the ferry to the hotel calls out from the front door. "I'd be happy to take you to your new destination."

A brightness kindles in Trina's gaze. She lifts her chin. "I'd rather walk."

Challenge accepted. I hold out my hand to her. "As you wish, Mrs. Ashley."

She flushes at the name and avoids my hand. "You didn't have to carry me." A beat of silence passes before she continues. "But thank you for taking care of me."

"That's not what you expected me to do?" I hold the door open for her and blink at the sudden brightness. Without the lights flashing, the world rushes back in bold color. I'm excited to explore Nantucket with my wife.

TRINA

I swing my phone camera like an enthusiastic tourist, showing Melanie where we are. Melanie sits in a little box on my screen, and she squeals in delight. "Oh, Trina. It's awesome that you're at the same place Adam and I stayed for our honeymoon." She claps her hands like an excited seal. "You'll love the hosts. Say hi to Steve and Marg for me." Melanie touches her cheek. "Actually, I got pretty wild when I had amnesia. They may not have such fond memories of me."

I grin as I hold the phone higher. "I'm sure they'll be glad to hear from you."

Liam touches my elbow. "Watch your step."

I make my way up the stairs to the Rose Resort path. Liam peeks over my shoulder and waves to Melanie. "Hey, sis."

I roll my eyes and elbow him, holding back my laughter. The guy can be amusing at times. But I'm not buying it. He wants me to change that article. He's sucking up big time and thinks I don't know. I'm a reporter. Nothing gets past me.

Rose bushes line the sidewalk which divides the beach from the resort. "How amazing is this? Right on the beach."

"Yeah, it's great," Melanie says. "Make sure you use the pool's hot tub at night. All the fairy lights in the trees make it so romantic."

I widen my eyes at Melanie. Hello? Remember it's only a game?

Voices mumble behind us. "Hey, Liam. Trina." The head cameraman waves for us to stop.

I hold up my hand in acknowledgement before focusing back on my sister. "We've got to go and perform again. It's so unnatural. They stop us over and over, doing retakes. Our walk took thirty-minutes. Should've taken ten."

Melanie gives me a sympathetic smile. "Now you know what it's like on the other side."

I shrug. "I guess I can empathize with the famous after all this." I side-glance to Liam. Except him. I can't allow any feelings for Liam. He would exploit any crack in my armor to win the war.

I end the call and the two cameramen approach. Anthony waves his fingers at me. "I'll interview you, Trina. Joel will speak with Liam."

Here we go. We've done this before. All part of the show. They pull us aside, expecting us to confess our true feelings for each other in front of America. I'm not an ignoramus when it comes to reporting. They will cut and edit the footage to suit their tactics for better ratings. Last interview, I froze, and they got little from me. The producer took me to the woodshed over it. He said I need to be more expressive and elaborate beyond two-word answers.

I follow Anthony around the bend, and we are shielded by a wall of roses. I can't see where Liam has gone. What will he say about me? He'll want to sparkle for his fans, so hopefully he won't be too negative. Will he lie and claim he's starting to fall in love? Ugh. I'll look like the mean one when we break up in three months. People come onto these reality TV shows with a strategy. I've been too busy planning a wedding and processing everything to think about mine. I guess I need to make that a priority now.

Anthony rests the camera on his shoulder and adjusts his lens. He peeks around and smiles. "Take a deep breath. Relax, Trina."

I shake out my arms. "Sure. I'm as relaxed as a jelly cup. Bring on the interrogation."

He chuckles. Anthony presses a button, and a red light comes on. "So, a fire alarm intruded on your honeymoon and made it necessary to switch hotels. How did Liam handle the situation?"

I blink, unsure of what to say. Have I said how much I loathe being in front of the camera? Unicorn-riding leprechauns will parade the streets before I ever get used to it. "Uh. I must admit, I was surprised. He took the lead and knew what to do." My neck heats at the memory of being tucked against his chest as he carried me. "He might have gone a little overboard playing heroic fireman, but . . ." I shrug. "I kind of liked it." What am I saying? I hope Liam doesn't see this. He will, of course. But when it's all over.

"You've only been together for a week. How do you feel toward Liam now that you've had a little bit of time together?"

My fake grin returns. "Well, it's not like we get a lot of alone time." I slap my mouth. "Sorry, am I allowed to say that?"

Anthony pokes his head around the camera. "Say what you want. We will cut out what's not appropriate."

I frown, not exactly sure of the rules, but anyway, it's out of my hands.

Anthony clears his throat. "Let me ask another question, then. Do you have any apprehensions about your first night together as husband and wife?"

I straighten. "I thought we were keeping things appropriate."

Anthony sighs. "I'm glad I'm not the editor." He shakes his head as he presses a button and lowers the camera.

"It's easy for you, Anthony. What if I had to ask you some personal questions. Tell me your deepest darkest secrets. Would you like those aired on national TV?" I plant a fist on my hip.

"Liam's got his work cut out for him—I can see."

I lean on my other hip. "Whose side are you on?"

He lifts a hand. "No one's. Shall we practice the questions off camera?"

Tension eases from my shoulders. "We can do that?"

"Sure. I understand you're nervous, Trina. That's normal. But you need to be open and honest as much as possible. It's part of your contract and it's what makes reality TV. Viewers like to know what's going on in your head. They need to connect with your heart. They'll fall in love with you if you're vulnerable."

"Oh." So, if I want them to favor me over Liam, I need to convince them I'm falling for him. Then when he dumps me, he looks like the big turd he really is. One thing wrong with that. I don't want pity. That would suck even more.

Anthony breaks me out of my reverie. "Are you okay with me asking for your thoughts about the wedding night?"

"No." I bark. "Hold on. They're asking Liam the same questions?"

He nods.

I cringe inside. I'm going to die of embarrassment. "Yes, just ask me. Like you said, I need to be a little vulnerable."

"Great. Let's practice." He grins. "So Trina, do you have any apprehension about your first night together as husband and wife?"

I smile. A genuine smile. "I can't wait, actually. I can't wait to see Liam's face when I ask him to sleep on the floor."

Anthony shakes his head and smirks. "We're not going to get anything deep from you today, are we?"

He adjusts his camera and resumes filming. We get through the questions in no time and return to Liam and Joel.

Liam grins wide as I approach him. What's he thinking? What did he say to Joel? Now is my moment to find out.

I skip toward him, matching his grin. "How did your interview go?"

He focuses on the path ahead as we enter the resort grounds. "Not sure if I should share that information."

I squeeze his cheeks and turn his face toward mine. "How did you answer question three?"

"Huh?" His brows scrunch inward before arching. "Oh, question three."

I drop my hand. "Yes. That question." My tone is low and full of sass.

He makes a squinty face like he's digging deep. "I said I'm looking forward to building a friendship with you."

I narrow my eyes back. "Sure you did. That's a good answer. Makes you seem like a gentleman."

Liam huffs. "I am. You believe I'm a player, but I'll prove to you I'm a decent guy. You don't trust me now, but I hope by the end, we can at least be friends."

I face forward. He's saying all the right things, but I've been here before. I've worked hard these last two years to ensure I don't fall for the wrong guy again. Liam will have several red flags. They'll start waving, soon enough.

Chapter 7

LIAM

A warm ocean breeze ruffles through my hair. I shoot a glance at Trina, who's bouncing down the sidewalk like she's stuffed full of sugar.

The image reminds me of her little nephew, Rex, and his near catastrophe with the cake. A laugh works its way up.

Trina whirls, hands on her hips. In an instant, she's ready to go toe to toe. I know basketball players with less grit than this reporter.

"What are you laughing at?" She glances left, then right. "The camera guys are gone."

I shake my head. "They went ahead so they could catch us with our mouths hanging open when we enter the resort."

She huffs and lowers her hands. "Right. Like they won't make us do it ten times if they don't like how we react the first time." She puts the back of her hand to her forehead and pretends to swoon. "Oh, Lawd. It's just ah-mazin'. Darlin, isn't it the best thing you've ever seen?"

A full belly laugh ripples out. "I'm not sure 'Southern belle' is the effect they're going for." I wipe tears from my eyes. "But you've nailed the dramatic flourish. Keep that up and you'll be fine."

"I'm already sick of this whole mess." She grumbles and kicks at the sand.

It's the most honest and vulnerable she's been this whole time. I stop her with a hand on her shoulder. "I was laughing because I remembered your nephew almost toppled our cake."

Her nose scrunches in an adorable pout.

"I have a nickname for him," I rush ahead before she thinks of something else. "Wrecking ball Rex." I pause and wait. "You think your sister would be offended?"

Trina's shoulders shake. Is she about to pummel me into the dirt?

Several heartbeats later, I realize she's laughing. She holds her arms over her stomach and bends at the waist. "That's the most accurate thing I've ever heard." Her laughter rings out bright and cheerful, a complete contrast to the grumbling I've been privy to since I picked her.

A sharp whistle cuts between us. Joel waves from the end of the path, then raises his hands in a *what's the holdup?* pose.

I take Trina's hand and squeeze when she stiffens. "Think of your favorite character and pretend they're the one on TV. Don't overthink it and try to have fun."

"Fun." She snorts and rolls her eyes.

We make our way closer, and genuine surprise forces me to stop. Trina does the same. The place is amazing. The brochure doesn't do it justice. Her head swivels back and forth. "Wow." We say it at the same time, then look at each other and burst out laughing.

Joel gives me a thumbs-up, his signal that we're good to go.

An older couple head our way and meet us at a rose-covered gate. "Welcome to the Rose Resort." The man holds out his hand. "I'm Steve, and this is my wife Marg."

We all shake hands and offer greetings.

Steve's smile grows brighter, and he sets off at a brisk walk down the path. "Trina, I understand you're Melanie's sister." He chuckles. "How's she doing?"

We keep pace with the resort owners. Fences line the sandy path. Roses bloom everywhere. No wonder they call it the Rose Resort.

Trina chatters away about her sister's amnesia.

I frown and try to remember if I knew about that. It's not ringing any bells. Then again, I didn't follow—or care about—her personal life until recently.

Marg stops on the stoop of a small beach house. She holds out the keys and jingles them. "Here we are." A twist, and the front door slides open. She motions for us to follow her. "There are cameras in the kitchen, living room, and dining room. Along with microphones." She points out the devices as we walk.

Trina's frown returns.

The place is nice, with an open area for dining and a smaller kitchen tucked away almost out of sight. A hallway extends in the other direction, and my throat seizes as I realize what's down there.

Trina and I share a look of suspicion once we take in the extent of camera coverage within the house.

She turns to Marg. "How did they install them so quickly?"

Marg fiddles with the keys, then passes them to me. Her cool fingers wrap around mine. She side-eyes Steve as he says, "Those guys are good at their jobs. Were in and out of here lickety split." He snaps his fingers and chuckles but it's a hollow sound.

Trina's hands pop onto her hips. First one. Then the other. It's cute the way she tips her head to the side and evaluates the setting. "And you had rooms for the crew on such short notice? There are a lot of them."

I like watching her treat this like an interview. Too bad she didn't give me the chance to speak for myself before she wrote my story. Or what she *thought* was my story.

"It all worked out." Marg shrugs, but her smile is tight. "We appreciate the business."

The whole exchange rings of a script being recited. Monotone voices and long pauses punctuate Marg and Steve's responses.

Steve claps his hands. "Who wants to see the pool?"

Trina raises a brow at me. "You up for a tour?"

I motion at my shorts and t-shirt. "I'm ready for a swim."

Marg hurries toward the front door. "You two are going to love it here. Melanie and Adam had such a wonderful time...once Melanie gave him a chance." She gives Trina a meaningful look.

I almost fall over backward. That'll be the day.

TRINA

There's a knock on the glass door. Behind it stands the head producer, Nicholas Parsons, and a herd of staff. How the heck will they fit into this tiny living room?

Liam opens the door, and they pour in like a fisherman's catch of sardines.

Boxes are plonked to the floor and two women start unpacking and decorating the living area. One places several scented candles on the coffee table and lights them one by one. Soon the place smells of cinnamon and orange peel.

Nicholas approaches Liam and me, placing a hand on each of our shoulders. "We'll make this as quick as possible and be out of your hair in no time."

Yes. It would be nice to get the parasites out of our hair. When do we get a minute to breathe our own oxygen?

Nicholas must sense my frustration. "I know it's been a long day. We only need two minutes of you eating a romantic first meal together, then a slow dance in the living room. We need to show you two connecting like the other four couples you're competing against."

I snap my neck backward. "What? We're competing against others?" I turn to Liam. "Did you know about this?"

He nods. "It's in the contract on how the show works. Didn't you read it?"

I shift on my feet. People bustle in and out of the door with boxes. I shake my head at Nicholas, wading through the fog in my brain. "What's the short version?"

"The network earns money from airing the show through commercials, but we also make money on the voting system. Each week, viewers call the voting line to choose their favorite couple. The fifty-five cents per call adds up to ... a lot. As in 100,000 votes equals

$55K. The winning couple gets a nice bonus at the end." He rubs his thumb against his fingers, enticing us with money, money, money.

Does money motivate Liam? His expression is flat. Perhaps he has enough, and he's not worried about a popularity contest. But me, I'm not rolling in cash. I could do with paying off my mortgage. Plus, I have a severe case of competitive-itis. When it comes to competitions, I need to win.

I turn to Nicholas. "How do we gain votes?"

Nicholas grins wide. "Now you're asking the right questions, Trina. Convince the viewers you two have chemistry. Have a lover's quarrel now and then but quickly make up. On the journal videos, pour your heart out."

I lift my hand like a stop sign. "The what?"

Liam wears a scowl, crosses his arms, and gives a dramatic sigh. What's his problem? "Every day, we have to enter a video booth alone and confess our true feelings about our spouse."

Nicholas nods. "That's right. Show the progress of the arranged marriage developing. In those moments, you can gain favor with the viewers if you're opening up and telling a story."

"A story?" My jaw hangs open. Did I land myself in *The Hunger Games* or something? Where contestants battle it out for matrimonial survival.

"Yes. You can create a story if you like. Only make it believable. People know it's reality TV and a lot of it's a setup. They put aside their disbelief and get sucked into the story. Escape their routine life and experience excitement through yours."

My eyes go wide. Wow. Half of America wants to live my life? Well, I'm more than happy to trade places. This one's too crazy.

"Think of the bonus money, Trina." Nicholas grabs my focus again. "And the thrill of winning in front of your family, friends, and the nation."

I missed out on a national competition due to my injury years ago. Sports reporting is now my go-to income, but if I could play state hockey, that's where I'd be right now.

Liam studies me. Judgment blazes in his eyes. Like, he's not all about competition? He's doing this for his team and sponsorship. The pot calling the kettle black

Nicholas pats our arms and turns away, giving direction to his crew of Martha Stewarts. They're hanging a picture of flamingo heads in the shape of a heart. Puke. Within ten minutes the table is set for two, complete with linen and candles. A fluffy burgundy rug and fake fireplace with glowing coals create a cozy atmosphere. The fireplace looks so real, like it was here the whole time.

Liam holds out his basketball hands to the fire and rubs them together. "Nice and cozy in here."

"Hmph." It's about as cozy as we'll get tonight. I hope he assumes that. Fake fire. Fake marriage.

He gestures to the table where a waiter stands, all-decked out with a cloth napkin draped over his arm. I follow Liam and when he pulls out my chair for me, instead of a dramatic eye roll, I flutter my lashes like I've got sand in my eyes. Liam gives a subtle shake of his head and smirks at my sarcasm.

Cameras swarm around us like bees in a hive. Overhead, soft lighting glows from the stands on the right, and reflector circles provide filler light from the left. TV viewers will only see the waiter and a married couple having a quiet intimate dinner. But in reality, nine people remain in the room. The interior decorators have left, but it still feels overcrowded.

Liam reaches across the table and squeezes my hand. "Ready to show America we're making a connection?" He delivers that sexy smile again.

I pull my hand away. "Yes. Give me a minute to get into acting mode." I sit taller and smooth the napkin over my lap. I take a deep breath and exhale slowly. I face Nicholas. "Ready for action."

He gives me a thumbs up and nods to the cameramen. Red lights blink on. Apparently, they only need two minutes of good dining footage, then we get a break. I can be nice to Liam for two minutes, no sweat.

I reach over and take Liam's hand. "Such a romantic dinner, isn't it?" I'm a writer. I know how to use words to set a mood. Using the word 'romantic,' will encourage viewers to believe we're for real. Hopefully. Perhaps I'll even convince myself. It's what I need to do—not merely play a role but become the character.

Ugh.

Liam places his hand over mine and massages the back of my wrist with his thumb. "It is."

Goosebumps climb my arm. The warmth of his palm creates tingles over my skin, and I shiver.

"Are you cold, sweetheart?"

I nearly choke out a bark of laughter, but I manage to keep it together. Sweetheart? Weird coming from Liam. He's not as great at this acting thing as playing ball.

I remove my hand from his. "I'm fine." The fake fire is creating plenty of heat.

The waiter pours sparkling grape juice into our wine glasses. Before filming, I told them I didn't want real wine. Water or soft cider will do. I plan to stay in full control of my actions both in front of the camera and behind the scenes. I touch my stomach. Just thinking about sharing a room with Liam makes me uneasy.

Dinner goes by fast. They only let us have a few bites of our meal. Gee, if this was a real honeymoon, it would totally suck.

In seconds, staff floods the space again and removes the food. We're escorted into the living area and situated before the fireplace. A make-up artist touches up my lipstick. Slow jazz plays, and everyone moves into position.

Nicholas steps forward. "Again, we only need two minutes of you having a first dance together. If conversation flows, we'll keep the cameras rolling. Adlib."

"Adlib?" I ask.

"Improvise," Nicholas says. "Show America you're connecting intellectually and emotionally."

"Right." Liam mumbles. "Easy to do with all of you in our faces."

I snigger.

Nicholas ignores Liam's complaint. Perhaps he didn't hear it. He waves for crew to zip it and pretend they're invisible. Silent descends except for saxophone.

Liam takes my hand and places his other palm on my back.

I grit my teeth. "I don't know how to dance. Give me any other sport, and I can do it. But dancing is not my jam."

His smile is warm. "Me neither. We can sway and talk."

I nod and let out a breath. Placing my hand on his shoulder, I ignore how solid his frame is. Good heavens, that's not an easy task. My hand itches to explore his bicep and tanned neck, but I squash the unwelcome temptation. Sure, he is my husband. I have a license to touch him, and he'd think I'm doing it for the show. But I would know. Bad idea. More than bad. Stupid.

In my peripheral vision, a cameraman moves around us, and the red light is on. I flick my bangs from my eyes and smile up at Liam. I hope he knows what to say. My mind is drawing a blank.

His grin comes easy. "So, tell me more about your life growing up."

What am I okay with America knowing? Not that I have anything to hide. I'm overthinking all of this and need to relax. "I lived and breathed sports. Field hockey was my favorite."

Liam raises one brow.

"I even made it into a state youth team." I glance at my feet, then focus on his shoulder. "But that year, I had a motorbike accident while on vacation. Trail bike. Campsite. Hit a rock and went head over heels. Broke my collar bone and fractured my ankle. Huge setback."

Liam pauses his movements. "Trina," he whispers.

I'm drawn into his green eyes. I find compassion there.

"That's terrible." His large palm moves to the center of my back like he's trying to steady me.

"Yeah. My family sacrificed years of weekends and drove me all over the country. They backed my future in hockey one hundred percent." I shrug. "Not meant to be, I guess."

"I'm sorry." He sways us into dancing again. "Did you return after you recovered?"

"They had to replace me for the season. Then I lost heart. Realized at any moment, everything could be lost. I decided to focus on my studies and chase a solid career. Aced my exams and got into..." The word "journalism" almost left my mouth. That's a detail I'd prefer America didn't know. There's likely a million Smiths out there, so I should be fine in keeping my Kat Smith reporter profile under wraps. "...something sustainable."

He nods as if my desire for secrecy is perfectly understandable. Once the producers found out I wasn't a real contestant, they didn't want it getting out that I was there that night by mistake. Well, not chosen by mistake. Liam purposely chose me for his own reasons.

"Enough about me." I smile. "Did you always dream of making it in the NBA?"

"Cut," Nicholas calls out. "Nice start people." He waves for the cameramen to change positions and he steps forward. Nicholas presses his palm against my back and moves me closer to Liam. "It's your honeymoon, remember. Time to move things along."

"Huh?" Liam frowns at Nicholas.

"Time for a little PDA. Since it's on national TV, it *is* public displays of affection, although you're hypothetically alone."

"Hypothetical. Ha." Liam shakes his head.

"What do you mean by PDA? What're you expecting us to do?" My tone reveals my annoyance. "I don't remember signing anything about this."

Nicholas tsks. "Section three. It's all there in black and white. You'll need to hug and kiss. Act like a newlywed couple."

"We kissed at the wedding ceremony," I say. "We're dancing. That's enough for one day."

"Section three, Trina. You signed it. Go read it later. Right now, we have a crew waiting." He waves his hands to the film crew inspecting their smart watches.

I stare at Nicholas. Seriously, buddy. You expect me to fake it with a guy I barely know and don't trust?

Nicholas huffs. "Fine. Tonight, just dance closer, cuddle a little. Do something." He rolls his eyes and steps back.

Liam radiates tension and avoids eye contact. He doesn't want to do this either. Nicholas really slapped a wet blanket over us.

"Is this the last take?" Liam asks.

"No. We have the hot tub scene next."

"What?" Both Liam and I answer simultaneously.

Nicholas waves his hands in the air. "Guys, it's your honeymoon. You're supposed to do romantic things together. It's costing a lot to have all this crew here. We want to get two days of filming in. Then we'll leave the rest to the journal videos and hidden cameras."

Liam straightens to his full height, towering over Nicholas. "Look. I'm tired. I'm hungry. We didn't get to finish our dinner. Let's move to the hot tub, so Trina and I can retire for the night."

I blink at Liam. I'm happy he's sticking up for us, though I'm not sure what he means by retiring for the night. I hope he means sleep.

Nicholas sighs. "Fine. Get changed into your bathing suits. Meet us at the pool in ten minutes."

Chapter 8

TRINA

I tiptoe barefoot across the cold pavement toward the pool, clutching a beach towel to my chest. Liam's already in the hot tub, the camera crew in position. If I could photoshop the film crew out of the picture, the resort is quite picturesque.

Melanie was right. The place is romantic at night. Green lights glow from the bottom of the pool. Fairy lights entangle the branches of several trees in the surrounding gardens. Bubbles foam over the surface of the hot tub and Liam's arms hang around the perimeter. As I get closer, I see his bare chest. No surprise, but good gravy, he looks amazing. How the heck am I going to fix my eyes on his face?

I cling to my security blanket, the towel that covers me from my armpits to my knees. Liam will not see me in a bathing suit. Half of America can see, but not Liam. The idea of him liking what he sees makes me want to run screaming. Attraction is not healthy for a fake marriage.

Liam waves to me and foam lands on his nose. He swipes it away, showing no sign of self-consciousness—unlike me. I give a small wave back and nearly drop my towel. I fumble to keep it high, this time clutching it closed at my neck.

Liam's smirk becomes a wide grin as I approach.

I stand at the edge of the hot tub, peering down at him. "Hi."

"Hi." He shifts across the bench seat. "Coming in or are you just playing lifeguard in case I drown?"

I lift my chin, and my ponytail flicks my cheek. "Can you face the other way while I get in?"

"Seriously? You're my wife, remember. Mrs. Ashley."

I roll my eyes. "Turn that way for a second."

Liam shrugs. "Sure." He turns and his back muscles flex.

The view does nothing for me. Zero. Nada. No attraction whatsoever.

I squat beside the steps and slip one foot in. Mmm. So warm. Still holding my towel, I decide America won't see me in my bathing suit either. I lower myself in, ready to fling the towel at the last second.

My strategy doesn't work.

My foot slides across the bench seat causing me to do the splits.

I let out a squeal.

My foot collides with Liam's thigh. I slip and go sideways. I brace for hard contact, but Liam's arm goes around my middle and pulls me into his lap. "Hey. Watch your step."

My heart is pounding in my ears. I catch my breath before I flick wet hair from my eyes. "Thanks for the warning." I wriggle the towel from under me and raise the drenched rag between us. "Looks like you're lending me yours."

His arms stay around my waist. "Ah. Not sure about that."

"What's yours is mine." I wave my wet towel. "And what's mine is yours."

"Oh, I see how this works." He smiles and tucks a wet strand of hair behind my ear.

Immobile at his gentle touch, I'm drawn into the depths of his mesmerizing eyes, where swirls of green and brown encircle dilated pupils. But a glimmer of an iridescent circle of light dances within his irises. Oh, yeah, the film crew stands behind us, and they've recorded my embarrassing stumble into the hot tub.

"Are you okay?" he whispers.

I bury my head into his neck and groan. "Tell them to go away."

Liam engulfs me in a hug, holding me close. "They'll leave in a minute. You can do this, Trina."

I pull back, our faces inches from each other. "I'm not used to this like you are. It's overwhelming. I want my privacy back."

"I get it." He cups my chin between his thumb and forefinger. "Let's give them what they want, then we can relax for the rest of the evening once they're gone."

I swallow. "Okay."

Liam presses his forehead to mine, staring into my eyes. "Okay? So you're ready?"

"Mmhmm." I'm not ready, but anyhow . . .

He lowers his head and nuzzles into my neck.

I giggle and squirm. "That tickles."

He mumbles against the skin below my earlobe. "Sorry. I wasn't going for laughter, but I'll take it." He chuckles.

I thread my arms over his shoulders and lift my head until our noses touch. "Thanks for helping me keep calm." I move to kiss his cheek, but he turns and captures my lips.

Sweet mercy. His lips are soft and wet from the water. His breath is minty and ohmygosh, I'm kissing him back.

I melt into his embrace, surrendering to this intoxicating man. His fingers gently trace the contours of my jaw, sending sweet shivers all over my body, and I find myself lost in the moment.

But I have to stop this.

Now.

I slowly inch back, ending the kiss before it gets any hotter in this tub. Our eyes lock, a kaleidoscope of emotions reflects in Liam's eyes—a mixture of surprise, desire, and an unspoken yearning for more.

I hide my face in his chest, regret flooding in. How could I let this happen? How can I backtrack what just transpired between us?

Pretend it was for show and didn't affect me in the least.

I whisper into his ear, "Can you tell them to go now?" I remain angled away from the cameras, mortified how our kiss was recorded. I can imagine Granny Smith watching us on TV. She'll likely applaud, but still, my whole family will see this with a bowl of popcorn on their laps.

Oh, I'm still sitting in Liam's lap. I need to move.

Liam calls over my shoulder. "That's it from us. Thanks for coming."

I laugh at this. But I stay hidden, my chin resting on his shoulder. As soon as the lights move away, I slide off Liam's lap and sit beside him. "Wow. We're good at this fake marriage thing. Nearly fell for it myself for a second."

Liam scrunches his nose and relaxes. "Yeah. Even had me fooled." He reaches for my hand under the water.

I dodge his hand and move further away from him. "Thank goodness the day is over. I'm drained." I wipe water from my brow. "I'm headed to the shower. Meet you back at the room."

"Oh. Okay." Disappointment lines his brow.

A pang of guilt hits me in the middle. I don't want to hurt Liam. Oh, flipping heck. I'm caring about him now. Not good.

I reach for his towel beside the hot tub and twist my body toward him. "Um. Can you look away again?"

His smile returns. "Sure."

"Thanks." I slip out of the tub, water sprinkling behind me. The weight of my body grows heavy as I step onto the tiles. Wrapping the towel around me tightly, I let out a breath. "You can look now."

Liam stands in the tub and his torso glistens from the glow beneath the waters. I'm staring. I know I'm staring, but goodness gracious me. How am I supposed to resist that tonight?

LIAM

Trina needs to stop looking at me like that. She took my towel, so I'm left standing, dripping, at the side of the hottub. There might be cameras out here. Probably not, but I'm not about to push my luck and say something I'll regret later when it's aired on national TV.

She's ridiculously adorable standing there wrapped in a fluffy towel up to her neck.

I'm tempted to grab it and give it a good yank, but considering she made me turn around before she'd get in or out of the water, I know she won't appreciate my attempt at humor. It's too bad, really.

I shake water from my hair and motion her to go ahead of me. "You can have the shower. I'll rinse off out here and meet you in the house." We need to have a serious talk about what's going to happen tonight.

Specifically what's *not* going to happen.

I rush into the pool shower and change into comfy jogging pants and another of my endless supply of t-shirts. The guys give me no end of heat over my attire, but I don't give two flying figs. I like my t-shirts. Nothing wrong with them.

I hear Trina moving around in the bedroom as I make my way through the living room and down the hallway. I avoid the cameras and try not to let it show that I'm running from their beady little eyes.

Trina gasps and grabs for the towel when I open the bedroom door. "Liam!"

"What?" Nothing's out of the ordinary.

She snaps the towel in my direction. "You scared me to death."

"Did not," I pop back at her while mimicking her hands on hips stance. "You're very obviously alive."

"You know what I mean." She smooths her hair and tugs a strand over her shoulder. "You said you would meet me inside."

"We are inside." I hold out my hands and peer around. "Did someone teleport us into another world where inside is outside?"

I shouldn't tease her, but it's so stinking fun. And now I know her cold looks and sass are hiding a gold mine of humor.

"You're ridiculous." She's dressed in flannel pajama pants and a long-sleeve matching flannel shirt.

I snort out a laugh. "Flannel? Really? And you call me ridiculous." I motion at her. "You're cute in flannel."

"What?" She plucks at the sleeve, all at once uncertain and blushing. "I didn't know how things would turn out and hotel rooms are always cold."

"And it's a good way to hide from your fake husband?" I keep my voice pitched low enough that the microphones can't pick it up.

She nibbles her lip but nods and tosses the towel into the hamper. Neither of us know what we're doing. This whole thing is spinning out of control. Trina didn't even read the full contract, which means she's in for a few surprises along the way. Like what happened today. "Look, we're in our safe place, okay?" I stretch out my arms. "No cameras, and as long as we're quiet, even the mics won't hear us. So, if there's anything that needs to be said away from the public personas we're playing, we'll do it here."

She nods once, the move precise and almost relieved.

I sit on the edge of the bed and pat the space next to me. When she shakes her head, I roll my eyes. "I promise I won't bite. We need to talk about tonight."

"Tonight?" Her voice squeaks. She takes a step back and clutches the shirt tight around her neck. "There's nothing to talk about. You're sleeping on the couch."

"No, I'm not." I need her to see reason so I go straight for the jugular. "If I sleep out there, everyone will see we're not taking this seriously. We won't get the votes. And we won't win." She gave me the key to success earlier and didn't even know it. I saw the gleam of competition in her eyes and heard it when she talked about playing field hockey years ago.

She wants to win. There are only a few ways we can make that happen.

I wiggle my eyebrows and hold up my hand in a stop motion. "I'll build a pillow wall between us. You won't even know I'm here." I jab my thumb over my shoulder. "They gave us a tiny house with a king-sized bed. It's perfect." I rubbed the back of my neck. "Plus, I'm way too tall for that couch. Did you even see it? I'd have a crick in my neck the rest of the week if I tried to sleep out there."

I watch her think it over. I could keep talking, but I'm too close to shooting myself in the foot.

Why risk it?

"I'll call Marg and see if they have a cot or something. I'll sleep on it and save your poor neck." She reaches for the phone.

"How will they get it past the cameras?" I flop backward on the bed and wiggle in deeper. "Ooh, it is a nice bed." With a kick of my feet, I scooch all the way up with my head on the pillows. My feet almost dangle off the end despite the enormous size.

Trina twists her hair into a knot at the base of her neck and eyes me like I'm a leper sure to give her cooties.

I stretch my arm out toward her side. "Look. There's so much space." I roll over onto my stomach and keep going onto my back again and I still haven't reached the other side.

Her huff of annoyance is enough to send me rolling back over. I snatch all the pillows except for the two we'll sleep on and pile them into a line down the center of the bed.

She watches me through narrowed eyes but doesn't argue. Wow. Small miracles do happen.

When I'm done, the bed is perfectly split between us. I lean back again. "I'll even sleep on top of the covers and you can sleep under them."

She picks at her flannel again and inches toward the bed. "You swear you'll stay on your side?"

I hold up my pinky. "Pinky promise."

Moving slower than a sloth in January, she hooks her pinky to mine and shakes it once.

That single touch is hotter than electricity zapping through my veins. I'm instantly awake. I hold my eyes half-closed so she can't see the intensity of my reaction to her.

Her gaze never leaves my face as she crawls under the covers and pulls them to her chin.

She'll roast under all those layers, but I keep my mouth shut. My interference is about as welcome as my touch. She doesn't want anything from me.

I lace my fingers behind my head to keep from pushing the pillows down so I can look at her.

"Will you turn off the light?" Her voice is muffled, sounding like she's already half asleep.

Wish I could say the same. I don't know if I'll be able to sleep at all knowing she's right there beside me. Closer than comfortable and yet completely out of reach.

Chapter 9

TRINA

The Nantucket beach stretches before me. The ocean's surface ripples like a sheet of pearl, and a fresh breeze cools my skin. Ah, a moment of peace. I cross my feet at the ankles, lean back into the porch swing, and open my laptop. After watching the sunrise, I'm prepared for whatever the day will bring.

Liam slept in, so I crawled out of bed nice and early to get some work done—without him knowing.

My pseudonym for the paper is Kat Smith which is an attempt to keep my journalism and personal life separate. Thanks to Liam who picked me for this show and disrupted everything, that's just gotten a whole lot harder.

My boss expects the second article this week. We decided on the pen name, M.J. Albert. Could be a female but sounds like a male. I wrote a three-hundred-word article about the opening night. Boss said it sizzled with emotional tension, and he loved it. Seems I write better when I'm the main character.

In this article, I'm M.J. Albert, enjoying the island and spying on the newlyweds. I tap out a few sentences:

To join in the intrigue and speculation surrounding the recent fire alarm incident on "Bride at First Sight", it's possible the show's producers orchestrated the chaos to test the resilience of the couple. It undoubtedly adds another layer of drama to an already tension-filled reality TV experience for Liam and Trina. I'd venture to guess there's more to the behind-the-scenes manipulation fueling the on-screen flames. Will the strain of these manufactured obstacles prove too much for the newlyweds?

The sliding door screeches behind me. My heart jumps in my throat, and I promptly open a new tab.

"Morning, wifey," Liam croaks.

"Morning, hubby nubby." I turn and frown at the state of him. "Gee. You look a little rough. Thought you'd be refreshed after a long sleep in."

Liam scrubs a hand over his face. He yawns and stretches his arms over his head, revealing a sliver of tanned flesh at his waistband.

I turn away and shut my laptop.

"What are you working on? You're supposed to be on vacation." Liam settles next to me, straining the swing. He pushes off the ground and we start swaying.

I clutch my laptop before it slips. "Checking emails and stuff. What about you? How long before you have to return to training?"

"As soon as we get back to the mainland. Five days for a honeymoon isn't ideal."

"No. But nothing about this setup is ideal."

Liam glances over his shoulder to the alfresco ceiling where a small 180 degrees camera sits. He lazily puts an arm around me and faces the beach. "Wonder what they have planned for us today."

"Mmm. Not sure." I allow my eyes to drift to a close for a moment. Liam's body heat and cologne make me want to cuddle into him. I could. He'd think I did it for the camera. But I'd be putting myself at risk. Gotta keep my head in the game, not my heart. He's competitive too, and he's trying to sweeten me up and win my favor, so I'll make that article disappear.

I should be trying to dig up dirt on him. I study his profile. "Before the show, how come you were single? When was your last serious relationship?"

Liam pulls back and places his hands in his lap. "Why the questions?"

I lift my chin, undeterred. "It's a normal question new couples ask their partners."

He crosses his arms. "You first."

"Oh, no you don't." I mirror his posture. "I asked *you.*"

Liam plants both feet to the floor and the swing stops. He rests his elbows on his knees and leans forward. "I haven't been in a relationship for two years. If the team has an event, I take a date. Often, it's . . . a close family friend." He angles his head toward me. "Your turn."

I wave a finger. "Not so fast, mister. Why did you break up with your last girlfriend?"

He sighs. "Because of me."

I blink. Here we go. Here's the dirt. He cheated, didn't he? I wave a hand encouraging him to keep going.

"I put my career before the relationship and couldn't give her what she needed. Quality time."

Oh. Not what I expected. Sounds truthful. I'm all too aware of the demands on professional players.

"Now it is your turn." He grins.

I dived into the subject without thinking this through. But it's only fair that I open up in return. "I had a three-year relationship with . . . let's just say he's a professional athlete, no mention of what sport since he's got a name for himself . . . in more ways than one." I sigh heavily. "He cheated on me twice. First time, he said it was only a drunken kiss at an after-game party. Second time, well . . . I wasn't as willing to forgive and forget."

Liam places a hand on my knee. "Sorry he did that to you. He's the loser. You're better off without him."

The back of my eyelids burns, and I blink to chase away tears. Liam's affirmation means something. Maybe because he sees this behavior of cheating on partners more than most.

"I guess you swore off dating professional athletes?"

I nod.

"We're not all like that, you know. At least I'm not."

I get the urge to ask him about the night he took a drunk girl to his place. I did some investigating before I published the article. It had to be a one-night stand because he wasn't in a relationship. Liam took advantage of her inebriation. I won't bring it up now. The camera over there might have a supersonic mic for all I know. Plus, picking through that mess could initiate a big argument. We need the viewers to believe we'll last, so we must appear like we're getting along as much as possible.

I stand. Aqua waters spill onto the sand ahead. "We'll see. Like those foaming waves—the truth will wash to the surface in the end."

LIAM

No way. I angle a look at Trina, then at the twin jet skis sitting on the water. It's a beautiful Nantucket day. Are there ever any bad days here? I've checked the weather forecast and it's perfect temps and blue skies all week. But this puts a bit of a damper on the day. I knew they'd give us challenges to complete, but I didn't expect this.

"You're joking." Trina plops her fists on her hips and glares at the producer like he has spikes growing from his forehead. "A relay race?"

"Yep." The man is practically giddy. He rubs his hands together and then motions around us. "You ride the jet skis out to the buoy, go around the far side and over to the mini cat." He holds up a finger. "You each must ride your own jet ski but work together to sail the cat. You sail it back here within the allotted time and you win a reward. An overnight stay on Nantucket Dreams, the finest yacht on Nantucket. It also comes with a luxurious dinner."

"And if we fail?" That's the part I'm worried about. Trina and I are both super competitive, but I'm not sure of her skill on the water. This whole thing could be over before we ever get started.

She shoots me a dirty look. Great. Add me to the list of people she's mad at. This day will be so much better.

"If you lose, you spend the night camping. In a tent. With nothing to eat but baked beans." The producer shakes his head side to side. "We don't want that." He's playing it up for the cameras perched all around us.

I peel off my shirt and toss it onto the sand. Thumbs pop up from the surrounding crew, which I try to ignore.

Trina's over there expelling long-suffering sighs like she's sure it will annoy me. I smile and hold out my hand. "How about it?"

She puts her palm in mine and holds tight as we run into the waves. I boost her onto her jet ski and secure her life jacket.

"I'm sure we'll get lots of likes for this wonderful fashion statement." She points at me and glares. "Don't fall behind."

Well, okay then. "I wouldn't dream of it." I sling my leg over my jet ski and fire it up.

We set off at the same time and point ourselves at the red buoy bobbing in the distance.

All at once, Trina's engine sputters. She veers hard right, going away from me. "Hey!" Her voice carries over the water in a screech. "This thing is busted."

"You both have to make it to the cat on separate jet skis," the producer shouts into a megaphone. Trina corrects her trajectory and zooms back toward me.

Too fast. Way too fast. If one of us doesn't do something quick, we'll crash. I push my jet ski to its limit and get ahead of Trina seconds before she cuts through my jet ski's wake. That was close. Too close.

She slaps her palm against the handlebar. "Stop it."

"It can't hear you." I circle around beside her. "Come on, let's switch."

"I'm telling you, this thing is broken. Every time I get close to passing you, it takes off on its own." She glares over her shoulder, lasering the men on the beach. "They're sabotaging us."

"Nah." I tug her closer and swing over behind her. "Go on. Take mine. We need to hurry and win. I'd rather not sleep in a tent tonight."

She grumbles, but trades places and we're off again. Foam spouts behind us as the jet skis fly over the blue water. I can't find a single thing wrong with her jet ski. It rides as smooth as butter—well, as smooth as a jet ski can.

Trina zooms past me, a tight smile pulling at her lips. "First one to the buoy doesn't have to cook dinner tomorrow." Her laughter matches the bouncing rhythm of her jet ski.

I smile at the sound and ease off the gas so she wins. I'm a sucker for a woman's laughter. Like most men, I can't handle tears, but laughter gets me into all sorts of trouble. And Trina has a great laugh. It lights up her whole face, especially when she tips her head to the sun. For the first time, I see how free she can be when she lets herself forget about the cameras and has fun.

We round the buoy and aim for the cat. The smallish boat is similar to one I've used before, so I'm confident I can get us to the end under the allotted time.

I'm not sure how much longer we have.

I hop onto the mini cat and hold a hand out to Trina.

Her expression is a thunderstorm of annoyance. "Someone rigged that jet ski. The minute you hopped on, it drove fine." She drops onto the side pontoon and crosses her arms.

"No time to pout." I settle at the rudder and motion at her. "You need to man the lines. Keep wind in the sails."

"Huh?" She scans the boat, and her eyes shoot wide. "I don't know how to do any of that." She moves beside me and shoves my shoulder. "I'll steer. You do it."

"Do you know how to steer?"

She shrugs. "Can't be that hard if you know how to do it."

"Har har." I let her swap places with me and move to man the sails. "We'll need to shoot straight for the beach."

"Yeah, yeah." Her brows pinch together as she concentrates. She pulls on the rudder and the cat spins. "Whoa." She lets go and lifts her hands. "This thing is crazy sensitive."

"Yep." I gather the lines. "Want me to do it?"

"Let me try again."

Seconds later, we're going nowhere. Trina pinches the bridge of her nose. "This is ridiculous. How are we supposed to win when everything is rigged to make us fail?"

"Switch back. I'll help you." I point while nudging her out of the way. "Pull that line tight."

Trina grabs the rope and hauls it back. It's too much too quick. The cat swings sideways as the wind grabs the sail and drags us around.

I shout a warning too late. Trina is in the air, arms and legs flailing. Then she's in the water, splashing straight down and sending water cascading over me.

Seconds later, she breaks the surface, swims back to the cat, and climbs aboard. We're not wearing microphones because of the water, but I can't be sure there aren't any on the cat.

Why is Trina holding back?

"Great. Flipping fantastic. I'm sure to look like a drowned rat on national TV. And that's *after* I slip and almost fall into the hot tub." She squeezes water from her hair and flips it over her shoulder. "This one is all yours, hot shot. I'm done."

She's giving up? "You don't want to win?"

She waves a hand toward the beach. "We lost. Timer went off about the same time I hit the water. I saw it flashing as I hit."

I follow her pointing finger to the big red zeroes flashing on the beach. Great. Guess we're camping.

We limp onto the beach and slide out of our lifejackets. The cameramen swoop in on us, and I squeeze Trina to my side as a warning not to react. Her bathing suit flexes with her deep inhale, and she caves toward me. Uh oh. A delighted smile breaks free. "You're ticklish."

"Am not." She inches away from my probing fingers. "Stop it."

"Nuh-uh." I dig my fingers into her ribs.

She breaks away from me with a squeal and runs up the beach.

I follow, my hands stretched out like claws. "You better run faster. You're sleeping in a tent with me all night." I pause for dramatic effect. "After I've eaten beans."

Her laughter bursts out in that amazing sound that reaches all the way to my bones. I put on a burst of speed and snap both arms around her waist.

With a sliding stop and a twist, I pull her off her feet. She kicks and screams while laughing and slaps at my hands when I tickle her again.

"Don't." She kicks my knee with her heel. "Stop."

"Don't stop?" I breathe in the scent of sun-warmed skin and a unique scent that is all Trina. Intoxicating. "Okay. I won't stop."

She screams louder and flails. "I'm going to get you for this," she says between spurts of laughter.

I lower her to the ground. "Oh, I hope you do."

Chapter 10

When they said we'd be camping, I expected a tiny tent and not much else. Trina and I walk from the rose-lined path onto the beach, and I stop dead in my tracks.

A round yurt sits several yards away, the flaps pulled back to reveal a modest interior. There's a ring of stones, and Trina heads that way.

Nantucket is warm and cheerful during the day, but there's a bit of a chill to the night air. I'm grateful for the chance to sit by the fire.

Trina drops to her knees by the stones and glances at me over her shoulder. A grin brightens her eyes. "You know how to start a fire with these?" She holds up several tools I can't even identify.

I shake my head and sit cross-legged in the sand beside her. "My style is more push a button and wait for the whoosh."

She curls her nose. "You mean a fake fireplace?"

"Or a gas one," I protest. "They're great." I mimic Tony the Tiger from those cereal commercials, rolling and drawing out the "r" until Trina rolls her eyes.

"Guess it's finally my time to shine." She keeps her gaze averted from the blinking cameras. They're far enough away we can almost forget they're there. Almost.

I lean forward and prop my elbows on my knees then set my chin in my cupped palms. "Teach me, oh wise one."

"I will." Her tone is smug as she rips a tube of fibers into thin strands, then takes one of the tools and shaves off tiny slivers. "Magnesium. You want it to sit on your fire starter. You need tiny pieces to start with. Dryer lint is a great fire- starting material." She concentrates on the pile in front of her while she continues. "Once it's

81

lit, you slowly add your bigger pieces. Add too much and you'll smother it."

"Hmm, sounds like a romance story to me." I try for playful, but Trina is too busy to pay me much attention.

She strikes the two pieces together and sparks fly.

"Holy mackerel." I lean back and pull my ankles away from the pit. "I didn't mean it."

"What?" She strikes again. Sparks rain onto the magnesium and the fluff she called fire starter. "Oh, the romance thing." A gleam enters her eyes. "One where the guy smothers the woman in her sleep, maybe."

"You're harsh."

She lifts a shoulder. "I prefer realistic."

I remember what she said earlier about her previous boyfriend. I can't imagine treating anyone like that, much less someone I was into.

Trina holds her hair at the nape of her neck with one hand and leans down to blow on the sparks. Smoke billows in a tiny tendril, then blooms into a crackling flame. She whoops and grabs my arm. Her excitement is contagious and without thinking, I lean forward to kiss her cheek. "You're amazing." I mean it too. She's a one-of-a-kind woman any guy would be happy to spend the rest of his life with.

As long as they didn't mind her publishing trash articles with no context or truth. I reel myself in before I'm lost in her gaze.

I know who Trina really is under the laughter and the fire-making skills.

Her smile dims. She blinks like she's coming out of a trance and ducks her head. Her hair falls in a curtain between us. "Let's see what they gave us for dinner." She stands and brushes sand from her legs.

I move to follow her, but she waves me back.

"Let me handle this." Her voice is back to carrying an edge.

Shoot. I messed up. Again.

She rummages around in a cooler and comes back with several packages. "I can make this work."

"What can I do to help?" I hate sitting here like a knot on a log. I'm not accustomed to being useless. My team counts on me the same way I count on them. We wouldn't win the way we do otherwise. Even as a kid I learned how to pitch in and help around the house. I know how to cook a few basic things and clean up after myself.

Getting into the NBA didn't change who I am at my roots.

That's the person I need Trina to see. If she'd believe me, I'd flat out tell her right now her article was garbage. But she won't believe me. Not yet. I haven't earned her trust.

Why does it matter so much? Maybe it wouldn't if I knew I could let this whole thing go. It's not like we'll have anything to do with each other once this marriage sham ends.

Trina hands me two ears of corn with the husks still on. "Stick those at the bottom of the fire. Not directly in the flames."

I do as she directs then sit back to wait for my next order. Nantucket nightlife is minimal. Maybe because of the fire. I bet the crew set up deterrents. They wouldn't want any critters sneaking up on them while they film. Now that would be great reality TV.

Time ticks past in a slow cascade, almost like it's nonexistent here on Nantucket. Trina does her magic on the food, and soon I smell an amazing aroma.

"Where did you learn to do all this?"

She brushes her hands over her thighs and sits beside me. "I grew up camping. Dad loves the outdoors. He took us out in the woods every chance he got. Taught us how to cook outside, start our own fires. This is like being back home." Her voice hitches.

I reach out to comfort her but drag my arm back. Stupid cameras. They have my emotions in a jumbled mess. I should comfort her for the show, but I want to do it for myself, and that's a slippery slope.

I can't fall for Trina. How ridiculous is that?

The fire crackles and pops, sending sparks into the sky.

"Could you help me with something?" Trina stands and makes her way toward the yurt. We step inside and she closes the flaps. She leans in close and lowers her voice to a whisper I have to strain to hear. "The race was rigged. I can't tell you how I know, but I know. And I'll prove it. Those buttons were tampered with, but then they worked fine for you. It's suspicious."

I want to argue with her, but she has a point. Her jet ski worked just fine for me, and she operated mine without any trouble. I wouldn't put it past them to rig the race. "Well, camping is more romantic."

"Than a yacht?" Her nose scrunches and she raises her voice. "Yeah, that's great, Liam. Bring those pillows." She motions toward her ear, like she expects someone to be listening in, then turns away, leaving me gaping after her.

I grab pillows and follow her back to the fire. I give her one and sit on the other while she fishes our dinner out of the fire.

My stomach rumbles. I retrieve the roasted corn and set it aside to cool. Trina peels back the aluminum foil and hands me the packet she assembled.

"We called these campfire scrambles. Basically, you take everything and throw it together in the pouch, then roast it."

"That's great, guys." The voice comes out of nowhere, then Joel steps into the firelight. "We'll leave you two alone now. There's a couple of cameras focused on the fire and the surrounding area, but the yurt is camera and mic free."

Great, they didn't catch what Trina said.

What, exactly, does she plan to do with the information she digs up?

TRINA

Thank goodness the camera crew checks out today. They've stopped swarming around us like pesky flies. The unit remains bugged, but outside we're free.

Liberation rushes through me as I practically skip to the beach, kicking sand.

The breeze fingers my hair and the sweet scent of sunshine and salt lifts my mood.

"Wait up, buttercup," Liam calls behind me.

Oh, him again. That's right, I have a fake husband hanging around 24/7. Not so free after all.

I slow my steps, turn, and shield my eyes from the afternoon sun. "Hurry up, then."

He catches up and keeps with my pace. "What's the rush?"

"There's no rush, I'm just eager to talk to the lady who leases the jet skis. See if anyone else has had problems."

"Always the reporter." He smiles.

I give him a once-over. His t-shirt is too tight. The image of Liam in the hot tub, droplets sliding down his chest haunts me every night as I try to fall asleep.

Liam's lips quirk to one side and he circles his chest. "Liking what you see?"

"Excuse me?" I wince like I've swallowed a mouthful of sand.

"You're staring at me again."

I jab at his pectoral. "You have a stain, buddy."

He dips his chin. "Where?"

I smack his mouth and set off running.

"You little—!" He yells as he chases after me.

The wind tosses my hair, and a bubble of laughter rises in my throat. I'm a fast runner, and I keep fit. Wouldn't it be hilarious if I beat him in a race? If only the cameras could record this.

I've gained some ground, but his pounding steps thump close behind. The guy's long legs give him the advantage.

"Gottcha!" Liam yanks me into his chest.

My feet leave the ground, and I squeal.

Liam topples backward. His arms instinctively tighten around my waist before we hit the sand. He lands first with a thud, and I collapse onto him, the breath forced from his lungs.

Oh, that didn't sound too good. I roll in his arms to face him. His eyes are shut, and Liam groans.

I swipe sand from his forehead and brush it from his hair. "You okay?"

He cracks one eye open and his large hands smooth over my back. "Worth it," he croaks.

"Worth puncturing a lung?"

"Yep. At least I beat you at something."

I tsk. "Husband dearest, let me enlighten you with my extensive research on this whole marriage thing. Lesson number one: The wife, in her infinite wisdom, gently strokes the man's ego, allowing him to bask in the illusion of having a win now and then, all while she quietly pulls the strings of marital control."

His chuckle bounces me upon his chest. "Sweetheart, you've just revealed your strategy. So it's checkmate, my queen."

"Sure. Keep thinking that. It's exactly what I want." I push up from his chest, dust the sand from my shirt, and offer a hand to Liam.

He takes my hand and pauses. "My ego's not so big that I can't receive help from my beautiful wife."

My smile falters. There are no cameras or mics today. Why does he have to say things like that? I'm not beautiful. I'm a reporter who's going to expose his biggest secrets. "Come on, you big lug. Get up. I have some investigating to do." I struggle to heave him upward but hide my strain.

We return to a brisk pace, and I spot Samantha winding a rope on the dock.

"Nantucket Dreams." Liam points to the yacht. "We should get Samantha to take us out on the water." He winks at me. "We won't let you steer."

I shove his shoulder. "The mini cat might've been rigged too."

"Doubt it."

We reach the dock and make our way down the jetty. I wave to Samantha. She smiles at first then darts a glance everywhere but at us. I've taken courses in body language. It's helpful to read people when I interview them. I'm no expert, but I can pick up avoidance cues.

"Hello. Samantha, how are you?" I ask, a little breathless.

"Hey, guys. No camera crew today?"

"Nope. Thank heavens," Liam says.

"What's it like being on a reality TV show?" She pushes blonde strands behind her ear.

Liam scrubs more sand out of his hair. "We're slowly getting the hang of it. Coming to Nantucket has been a treat. And you get to enjoy it every day."

"Yep. This place is pretty amazing. I spent half my childhood here on vacations then started a business on the island. I'm Steve and Marg's niece."

I perk up at this bit of information. "Really?"

"Yeah. And my cousins live here too. Ellie runs the bakery in town. You've got to try her cinnamon rolls." She kisses her fingers. "Baked to perfection."

My mouth instantly waters. "We'll go there next." I shift on my feet. "Hey, I wanted to let you know I had problems steering my jet ski. Funny thing though. It worked fine for Liam when we swapped."

Samantha dips her chin and scuffs her shoe. "Not sure what happened there."

I lower my voice. "We're not wearing any microphones. I just want someone to tell me—rather Liam here." I elbow-nudge him. "I'm not crazy. Did the producers rig the jet ski?"

Samantha slowly raises her head. "I can't say. They aren't my jet skis. The TV guys brought them over from the mainland. Not mine to lease."

I grab Liam's arm and give him a little shake. "See. I knew something was sus."

He frowns. "It doesn't prove anything. Who's to say they meant the jet skis for anything more than the challenge?"

I turn to Samantha. "Were you watching?"

She gives a slight nod.

I can tell she knows something. "Do you think they could've been remote-controlled?"

Samantha shrugs. "It's a possibility."

I rub a hand across my chin. "I'll have to keep digging then."

She gives me a sympathetic smile. "Hope you find what you're looking for."

We leave Samantha and head into town.

The cobblestone street creates a Christmassy feel though it's early summer. "I love these quaint little stores." I point to the art and craft shop, spilling color onto the street with display stands of tie-dye sarongs, t-shirts and caps.

Liam gestures to the bakery. "Sweet By Design. That must be where Ellie works."

As soon as we enter, vanilla, strawberries and the aroma of coffee hits my senses. "They should call this place, Sweet Heaven on Nantucket."

Liam places a hand on my lower back as we approach the counter. The touch should irritate me, but it doesn't this time.

A young woman bearing similar features to Samantha greets us with a glowing smile. "How can I help you?"

"Ellie Jones?"

Her brows go up. "Yes. Well, I'm married now. But originally a Jones."

"Sorry, I should introduce myself." I hold out a hand over the server counter. "I'm Trina Smith." I look at Liam. "And this is my husband, Liam."

Ellie shakes my hand. "Nice to meet you."

Liam leans into me as he whispers to Ellie. "She's Trina Ashley now. We've only been married a few days."

My cheeks go hot. "Oh, yeah. Sorry, honey." I grit my teeth at Liam.

"Anyway," I continue, "we're staying at the Rose Resort. I believe your family owns the place."

"Yes. Marg and Steve are my parents."

I nod. "Have you heard that there's a reality TV show being filmed on the premises?"

"Yeah. They've been preparing for months. They're hoping the publicity will bring a tidal wave of reservations."

I try not to show my surprise. "Right. So they've had months to get the place up to par?"

"Yes. Dad has been manicuring those rose bushes like they're bonsai trees."

"His work has paid off. They look amazing." I scan the display cases of sweets. "Anyhow, we heard this place served the best cinnamon rolls on the planet."

Ellie laughs. "This is true."

I smile at her. "We'll take a tray of your finest selection, please."

She's given me everything I need to know. The producers did set up the fire alarm debacle. Come to think of it, there were no other guests pouring from the building. This confirms my speculations, and now I can plunge into a new article about the remote-controlled jet skis.

My boss is going to be over the moon when there's an impressive surge in online views and subscriptions. The traction we're getting will pave the way for something big. When the show reaches its finale, I'll have the leverage I need to make my case for a well-deserved promotion.

Chapter 11

TRINA

I flop onto the couch, snuggling into the cozy cushions with a bowl of popcorn in one hand and the TV remote in the other. We're celebrating the camera crew's departure by watching a rerun of a Thunderhawks' basketball game.

The star of the show is sprawled out like a lazy lion. The guy is massive. I tuck my legs under my thighs to create some space between us.

"I'll give you some pro tips," I say before shoving a handful of popcorn in my mouth.

Liam laughs to the ceiling.

I give him the wife glare. Melanie told me it's about time to try out the superpower bestowed on me when I received the golden ring. Apparently, all married women have this ability, and now I get to use it.

I squint and tighten my lips until they fold inward.

Liam's face morphs into a mix of panic and regret.

It's working. Without me having to say a word, he knows he needs to back off and beg for mercy.

His eyes widen. "Got a kernel stuck in your throat?"

I huff and slap my hands on my thighs. "No, I don't."

His frown deepens. "What's wrong, then?"

"It's the wife glare, dummy. Don't you know anything?" I can't help but crack a smile.

"The what?"

"That one look which enables you to read my mind. Like if you leave your boxer briefs on the bedroom floor. I just need to stare at said underwear, and you'll fall over yourself rushing to pick them up."

"Who told you that trash?"

I cross my arms. "I'm probably not supposed to explain it to you. I'm obviously doing it wrong and need to watch some YouTube videos or something."

"No, you were doing it right. I got scared for a second there. Now that I know what it means, I'll perfect the art of trembling under your Medusa glare."

"Good. An important part in sweet marital bliss, dear husband." My tone drips with playfulness. "But don't worry, I will save the wife glare for special occasions. It shall be wielded wisely."

Liam nods. "Absolutely, my love. Consider this my official apology." His brows scrunch inward. "Remind me. What am I apologizing for?"

A burst of laughter escapes my lips. I shake my head and press play on the game. "I'll send you some YouTube videos too."

We settle into watching the game. Liam picked one where they ended up winning, of course. I've seen this match before, and a week ago, I would've been hissing through my teeth each time Liam had the ball. But now, I'm admiring his skills. And that's not all I'm admiring. My husband is a bit of a hotty, especially red-faced and sweaty. Still smoking hot.

What am I thinking? He's not a real husband, Trina. And he's not really yours.

Screeching of sneakers, umpire whistles and cheers from the crowd emit from the surround sound system.

Tandy, one of Liam's teammates, slaps the ball, but hits the opposition's hand in the process.

"Are you serious?" I yell, my voice tinged with disbelief.

"What?"

"The ref didn't call the foul." I sit upright.

"There was no foul. The other guy was faking it. Tandy didn't touch him."

"It's right there on video."

"Trina, I was there. It didn't happen."

"And you remember every second of the game? Let's see if you were even looking." I wave the remote. "Rewind."

His team member committed a blatant foul, and Liam is too blinded by his biased loyalty to admit it. Why can't he just swallow his pride and acknowledge the truth?

Liam looks at me as if I'm out of my mind. "It was a clean play, Trina. The umpire made the right call, trust me."

I throw my hands up in exasperation. "Clean play? Liam, are you watching the same game? That was a textbook violation, and you know it."

He shakes his head with a chuckle, as if my words are nothing more than a whimsical tale. It's infuriating. "Trina, come on." He leans in and whispers. "Just because you're a sports journalist doesn't mean you know the ins and outs of the game."

My jaw drops, and my face burns. I point the remote and rewind the game. I scroll through settings and change the playback to 0.5X.

"I know something about basketball, Liam." My voice is laced with determination.

He raises an eyebrow, his expression so smug. "Prove it."

The video rewound too far, but I use it to my advantage. With each play that unfolds on the screen, I give a commentary, breaking down the strategies of each team and dissecting every pass.

Liam's jaw drops slightly as he sits on the edge of the sofa, nodding and mumbling words to himself like, "Yeah. She's right."

I pause the game just before Tandy's foul. "Drum roll, please."

He shakes his head. "I'll give you an hour massage if you're right."

"Har. Sounds more like a reward for you."

He doesn't look at me, but he's smiling.

"Foot massage," I say. "If I'm right, you must give me a thirty-minute foot massage."

He turns and chuckles. "Deal. And if I'm right, you have to give me one."

"You little stinker." I hold my chin high. "Fine. I'm going to win this argument anyway."

With a triumphant click of the remote, I say. "Eat your smelly gym shorts, Liam Ashley."

In slow motion, Tandy jumps, palm outstretched. His hands hang suspended in mid-air for a fraction of a second. And then, with a resounding impact, his hand makes contact with the opposition's wrist.

The opposing player's face contorts into a mask of shock and pain as if he's auditioning for a one-man Shakespearean tragedy, but the umpire gives a shake of his head and doesn't call the foul.

I press pause and wriggle my finger at the screen. "And look at you, Liam. You're not even watching the ball. You've got your back to them, defending number twelve."

Liam's mouth opens and closes before turning to me with a hint of admiration etched on his face. He musters a sheepish grin, his pride momentarily deflated. "All right, you win. I stand corrected."

I hug his neck and laugh too loud in his ear. "Lesson number two, husband dear. The wife is always right."

LIAM

I wiggle in the hard chair and look into the camera. I'm supposed to do my journal interview thing but all I can think about is how Trina called me out—and proved Tandy's foul.

There's no one else in the room with me, and I haven't started the recording yet. It's beyond weird sitting here, staring at a screen.

The interviews are fine. Fun even. I've learned how to think on my feet and tackle an interview like I would a bad play on the court.

Man, that brings me right back to Trina. Can't believe she was right about that play. I scrub a hand over my face, take a deep breath, and press the record button.

My bright smile feels fake, but I've used it enough in promo shoots I know it looks real.

"You won't believe how much fun I'm having." I lean back and cross my arms, making the muscles pop. It's a trick Cool taught me, and I'm not above using it. "Trina is definitely a surprise. I knew when I picked her that she'd make life interesting, and let me tell you, the woman is not afraid of anything."

I rattle on for a few more minutes, doing my best to make Trina sound good while steering clear of tender subjects like our sleeping arrangement.

Before I sign off, I follow through on the "be vulnerable" part of the interview. "You know, after my last relationship, I thought I'd never date again." It's true. I wince before I can catch myself and give a self-deprecating smile. "Trina's changing my mind. She makes me want to take on new challenges." I lean in close to the camera. "The honeymoon ends tomorrow, folks. Let's see what life throws our way once we're an old married couple." I wink and end the video.

It's not great but not terrible.

Trina has kept an eagle eye on our ratings, and I get the news through her. Our heads remain above water for now, but we're not making any huge splashes.

Leaving the booth, I grab my phone and head outside. I need to experience the ocean wind and dig my feet into the sand one more time before we head home tomorrow.

Home. Wow. I hadn't let myself think about it too much, but reality is barreling toward us and there's no escaping it.

I dial my brother Clay. He should be home right now, though that's not guaranteed. The hospital keeps him busy and he's frequently on call. Clay says he doesn't mind, and since he's not married, maybe it's his way of keeping busy. Like how I play and practice for hours on end.

The phone rings three times, almost rolling over to voicemail, when Clay picks up. "Hey, man. How's the honeymoon? Are you two having a good time?" His chipper voice booms through the phone.

I roll my eyes even though he can't see me and dig my toes into the sand. Waves rush up and swirl around my ankles. I'll miss this place. I slide my sunglasses over my eyes. "It's...complicated. Like, more than I expected. We're having a good time." For the most part. "Trina's not too thrilled with my attention." Time for a truth bomb. "I like her. I think this could really turn into something. But she has no intention of going there."

Clay knows about the article Trina wrote, and though I haven't told him everything about why I chose Trina for the show, I think he has a pretty good idea.

Clay makes a noise that could mean anything. "Well, you two are strangers. Not like you married your best friend or anything."

"Yeah, but I can't ever say or do the right thing. It's like she *wants* to pick a fight with me." I work my feet deeper into the sand and wait for a great pearl of wisdom.

I'll be waiting a while. Clay is as lost as I am when it comes to women and romance.

His voice trickles through the background noise coming through his phone. I've caught him at the hospital. "Listen, I only have a minute. They're paging me for surgery." His voice turns harried. "Liam, you're a good guy. Trina doesn't know that. She only knows what she thinks she saw with Lindsay."

I scrub a hand through my hair and try not to grimace at the reminder of the article that started all this.

"Why not tell her the truth and be done with it?" Clay asks.

"And risk Lindsay's defamation of character?" I lift a hand and let it fall to my side. "She won't believe me. I'm trying to earn her trust, but she's closed me out. If I tell her now, she'll think it's some kind of ploy to get her to change the article. Which is what I want her to do, but you'd think she'd believe me if I said, 'Hey, Trina, by the way, the woman you saw me with was my cousin Lindsay. I took her to my house to sleep off the alcohol and nothing happened because one, she's my cousin, and two, I'm not a creep.' You think she'd listen?"

The barrage leaves me breathless and I stop talking.

Clay is silent for a long minute, but I know he's there. I hear the hospital noises in the background and his measured breathing.

"Wow." Clay's voice softens. "You really care for her."

The truth hits me harder than a basketball to the head. "Yeah. We're like some tragic love story or something."

"Nah." Clay chuckles. "You'll win her over. Use that charming personality you're famous for. She won't be able to resist you forever."

His name is called again. I wave a hand, which is ridiculous because he still can't see me. "Go on. Save lives. My love life will still be a gaping wound when you get done."

"I could throw a stitch or two in there if it would help." He laughs. "Talk later."

The call ends without a real goodbye. It's how we've always been. He'll call me in a few days, or I'll call him, and we'll pick up right where we left off.

The screensaver on my phone flashes. I stare at it, reading the words over and over. NO RISK, NO REWARD.

What I'm doing is definitely a risk, but if Trina is the reward, then I'm all in.

Love is about taking risks. I've taken plenty of risks on the court but never for a woman. The stakes are high, but I'm not about to let this opportunity slip through my fingers.

Chapter 12

Our make-shift confession booth in Liam's apartment is really a half bath.

Sure, the network has done an amazing job of making this look like a place for kissing instead of pooping, but I still shiver.

Liam assured me that hardly anyone used the spare toilet, and he always had a cleaner come in every week. Now that the network has taken over our lives, a maid cleans daily. Won't complain about that one.

I peer into the camera lens despite the blinding lights. A red curtain hems me in, blocking my view of the "confession booth," the nickname I've given it, and a velvet cushion hides the toilet seat I'm sitting on.

This time, I'm looking forward to my journal video. At least I'll be talking to someone—kind of. We've been back on the mainland for six days, and Liam is out day and night, catching up on training and promotional gigs. What about "Bride at First Sight," Liam? Thought we were in this thing together.

Well, I'm ready to tell America my newlywed woes. I can use his absence as the reason we break up after the show. He'll look like the one who failed the marriage. That's if I don't find anything else on him before then.

I lean forward and press the record button. I take a deep breath and slowly exhale. "Today, I've come to the realization that Liam may be repeating past relationship mistakes. His basketball career consumes his life. It's been six lonely days for me. I've moved into his place, and nothing feels like mine. No wonder I'm homesick. Most of my family live in another state, and my friends are too far for a spontaneous shopping excursion or a cup of coffee."

I did go out alone, but some people have recognized me from the show. One woman approached me in the grocery store, asking personal questions like she knew me. It's so weird.

"This week has been a rude awakening of what my life could be like. Absent husband. What if I have children with this man? Will Liam be a team player at home?" Okay, so I'm being strategic here. I have no desire to have a family with him. He's not my future. I wouldn't trust him to be a faithful husband. Too many temptations within easy reach. I vividly recall the opening night of "Bride at First Sight" and how women hung all over him. Why does it make me sick thinking about it now? I hold my stomach and breathe again.

"America, what should I do? Do I try harder? Make him delicious meals? Go and watch him at his training sessions and wait in the bleachers for the crumbs of his attention? Ladies, what would you do? I've heard the first year of marriage is difficult, but how can we work on it if we don't spend time together? He's so tired when he gets home that he showers and goes straight to sleep."

All true. But here is where my strategy comes in. "But you know what? I believe in Liam and his career. I want to get right behind him and support him one hundred percent. I'm going to do everything in my power to make this marriage work. Do you believe I can do it? Are you all behind me?" Now here comes the call to action. I don't know if I'm allowed to do this, but the editor can take it out if it's not permitted. "Vote for us if you believe we can turn this setback into a setup for a successful marriage. Your encouragement means everything to me. Thanks for listening."

I switch off the camera and drop my head in my hands. Man, that took a lot out of me. Being vulnerable and open comes at a cost. But I see Anthony's point. I will see a return. A swirl of emotion stirs in my belly. Why is there moisture in my eyes? I'm not going to cry over Liam Ashley. He doesn't deserve it.

Maybe I feel like crying because I depended on him too much that first week. He got me through some tough moments when I wanted to give up. Now I must rely on myself. I've got to focus on the end goal. I will make this work for my career.

Time to write another article from M.J. Albert.

I STARE OUT THE WINDOW of Liam's high-rise apartment. The night-time traffic streams by in short bursts of light. Tires roar, then fade. Our dinner waits in the warm oven. The cameras need to see me making an effort, and although I'm annoyed that Liam is late again, it shows the viewers that he's the one letting the home team down.

The apartment door unlocks with a click. Liam's footsteps come down the short corridor. "Honey, I'm home."

Ugh. I hate it when he says that. It's for the show, and he's trying to keep up the façade, but it's so cliché.

"Trina, you here?"

I'm half-covered by the lace curtains. I keep staring out the window mesmerized by the lights.

The fridge opens, and I hear Liam drinking from the carton again. He's a true bachelor.

The fridge door closes, and footsteps pad the tiles. "There you are. How was your day?"

I half turn and shrug. "Pretty boring, actually."

He strolls through the living area and collects the remote from the coffee table, standing in front of the TV. "When do you start work again?"

I cross my arms. "My boss gave me two weeks off because he thought we'd still be on our honeymoon. He'll send me some work in a couple of days."

Liam throws the remote to the sofa and comes over to me. "Hey, I'm sorry I've been so busy. They're making me catch up for the five days I took off. Things will slow down soon, I promise."

I look away from him and stare out the window again. Action speaks louder than words. We'll see what happens.

Liam comes up behind me, wraps his arms over mine, and rests his chin on my shoulder.

I stiffen.

"You're angry at me?"

I stand taller. "No."

Liam brushes his lips against the crook of my neck. "Don't be angry with me, Trina. I'm sorry you've been bored. We'll have some fun together soon. I'll take you out somewhere nice for dinner tonight."

"Dinner is in the oven."

"Oh, you made dinner. What a good wife you are." He chuckles.

I tuck my arms closer to each other, barricading my heart from his charms.

Liam pulls back a few inches, tugs out his cell from his pocket, and holds his screen at an angle where only I can see it. "Saw this funny cat meme today. Thought you'd appreciate it."

It's a message from Nicholas Parsons: You guys aren't showing much PDA. Get to it.

I let out a heavy breath. So that's why he's cuddling me. "Funny. But I've seen it before." I can't even bring myself to act cheerful. There goes my plan to be all chirpy and sweet to Liam for the cameras. Now that he's here, I can't fake it.

Liam slips his phone away and resumes hugging me from behind. He whispers into my ear. "I'm going to kiss you now."

Oh, really? Right now, when I feel like total crap.

His back is to the cameras, so they won't see our faces. I turn into his arms, and I find hesitancy in his eyes.

Well, he has nothing to worry about. I'm not going to let him kiss me for real.

I slip my hand up his chest and carefully place three fingers over his lips. Before he can protest, I stand on tippy toes and start kissing the back of my hand.

Liam stills for a moment, but he soon works out what I'm doing. He moves his head from side to side like he's making out with me.

With my other hand, which the camera can see, I use my fingernails to trail up his spine and thread my fingers through his hair, twirling the end of his curls.

He mumbles against my fingers. "What are you doing?"

The microphones pick up all our conversations, so I need to play along.

I giggle against my hand. "Do you like it?"

He mock-growls. "Yes, I love it when you do that."

He's playing the game, but his husky tone causes a surge of unexpected flutters in my midsection.

Before I can regain my composure, Liam reaches between our bodies, his hand wraps around my elbow, and he guides my fingers away from my mouth. Our lips collide, and the world around me fades into a blur as he drinks me in like a thirsty soldier.

Liam's hands slip around my back, pulling me impossibly close, erasing every inch of space between us. I'm crushed against his chest, the heat of his body radiating through mine, igniting a fire I need to put out before we both combust.

His kisses are hard and fast, leaving me breathless. I stumble back, but Liam follows, unrelenting in his pursuit. I'm backed against the window, trapped between the glass and the overwhelming force of his desire.

"Liam," I manage, my voice barely a whisper, a feeble attempt to regain control. It comes out more like a groan.

If Liam needed any more encouragement, that must've been his confirmation to go for it.

The intensity of his kisses escalates. His fingers tangle in my hair.

I surrender to the wild storm forming within me, and let it carry me away. The barriers around my heart are no match for his all-consuming touch.

I melt into his embrace, losing myself in Liam. The intoxicating passion has been there all along, but I've squelched my desire for him.

But in this moment, I don't care about restraint. And by Liam's kisses, he doesn't either.

His arm hooks under my knees, and a swish goes through my belly as Liam sweeps me into the bridal position. I cling to his neck and my eyes flash open. Walking through the house, Liam continues to kiss me.

I try to speak low enough that the cameras can't hear me. "Where are you taking me?" But again, it comes out like a muffled groan.

I feel as weightless as a feather. Liam holds me in one arm as he thrusts open the bedroom door.

Oh my gosh. This has gone way too far. I need to reel it in.

He clicks the door behind us, and instantly I jerk my lips away from his face. I smack his chest. "Put me down, you caveman."

Liam stares at me, blinks, and then drops me to my feet.

"What the heck are you doing, kissing me like that in front of the cameras?" I gasp in a breath.

"Me?" He jabs a thumb at his chest and then points in my direction. "What were you doing with your nails all up my back and playing with my hair? You were testing my limits, admit it." He folds his arms across his solid chest. The one I was pressed against a minute ago.

"What? I just—"

He lifts his chin. "Thought I'd give you back some of your own medicine. See how you like it." He gives me a wicked smile. "And you did."

"Har. The only medicine I need is anti-venom serum for your mouth germs." I swipe my mouth dramatically.

He throws his head back and laughs. "Don't deny it, Trina. You enjoyed it if your moans were anything to go by."

I stamp my foot. "Moans?"

"Lower your voice, they might hear us."

"I wasn't moaning, I was trying to tell you to take a chill pill, buddy."

He laughs. "Don't worry. You've dunked a nice icy bucket over me. I'm so chill right now."

"Good." I cross my arms. "You're sleeping on the couch tonight."

"Huh?"

"There's no way I'm going to trust a barricade of duck feathers with a hungry wolf on the other side."

Liam laughs harder this time before lifting claw hands and baring his teeth. "Afraid that I'll huff and puff and blow the pillow wall down?"

It wouldn't surprise me if he tried after those kisses.

I waggle my finger. "No excuses this time. We were told we could have lover's quarrels and make up later. People are going to think we are doing stuff since you raced me into the bedroom. My grandmother watches this show."

He rolls his eyes. "Trina, we're married. No one is going to judge you." He rubs his chest seductively, wearing a smirk on his face. "How long do you seriously think you can resist this?"

"Pfft. Dreamer." I look away. He's got a point there, but I'm not admitting it. I face him with the wife glare—the only weapon I have left in my arsenal. "You're sleeping on the couch, end of story." I storm away and slam the bathroom door behind me.

Chapter 13

LIAM

I wake up with the worst crick ever in my neck. Sitting up, I groan and rub at the sore spot. Trina's anger last night still confuses me. Why pick a fight?

She enjoyed our kiss. *I* enjoyed our kiss...a little too much. Thinking about her is a bad idea right now, because my brain is fixated on repeating that experience. The bedroom door is shut, telling me she's still asleep.

I swing my legs to the ground and stand, arching my back to work out the kinks. Sorry, America. Nothing like a sleepy head to make women's hearts flutter. There's nothing cute or sexy about me in the mornings. I'm all bed head and shuffling feet.

Thank goodness none of that follows me onto the court. I can imagine what the guys would say.

Grinning, I head into the kitchen and grab the milk from the fridge. A sticky note grabs my attention.

STOP DRINKING FROM THE CARTON! Trina's loopy scrawl makes my grin widen.

Is that why she's been ticked off at me? I guess I've gotten a little too used to living alone. I need to learn how to share a space. I glance around the apartment and frown. Nothing has changed since Trina moved in.

I remember seeing her toiletries in the bathroom. A razor in the shower. But out here, where the cameras record every minute of our day, there's nothing. I don't like it. She has every right to take up space here. This is her home now. *For now,* I remind myself. We have three months together. Do I want to convince her to stick around?

It's too early for these heavy thoughts.

The bedroom door opens and Trina steps out looking fresh and beautiful. My heart thuds loud enough she might be able to hear it from across the room.

"Morning." I hold out the milk. "Found your note."

She wrinkles her nose and shakes her head.

"Still not talking to me?"

She shakes her head again, but a tiny smile lifts one side of her mouth.

I set the milk on the counter and move close enough to smell her shower gel. "I'm sorry. I'll try to be around more. We'll hang out. Do stuff together." I point at the living room. "And we'll start by making this place yours."

Her eyes brighten and I know I've said the right thing.

Before she can say anything, a knock pounds on the front door. "Morning wake up call." Nicholas sounds way too chipper.

He's up to something.

Trina hurries over and opens the front door, letting the producer inside with a smile. "Let me guess, another challenge." She pops a fist onto her hip. "Liam just offered to take me shopping. This better be a good one. With a money reward involved."

Okay, I didn't offer to take her shopping, but if that's what she wants, I'm game.

Nicholas hands Trina a stack of notecards. "This is our version of Truth or Dare. We can't ask you to perform any crazy stunts, so it's a bit tame." He wiggles his eyebrows and grins. "But we think you'll like it."

Trina glances down.

Nicholas slaps a hand over the cards. "Uh, uh, uh. No peeking. You're going to sit at the kitchen table with the cards between you. Whoever goes first flips over the top card. If they refuse to perform the dare, then the opposing player gets to demand a truth from them." He claps. "Easy peasy. Now. I brought breakfast, and you're welcome. Let's go. No time to lose."

A trio of caterers rush in with their arms loaded. They arrange covered plates on the kitchen table and hurry out again.

I'll never get used to that.

Nicholas arranges us at the table, with me sitting on one side and Trina on the other so the cameras can catch our expressions. "I'll buzz your phone when we're ready. Until then, sit tight."

Ugh. I'm getting tired of all the hurry up and wait garbage. I'm hungry and getting cranky.

Trina sits back and pushes her palms against the edge of the table. "What kind of dares do you think they gave us?"

I shrug. "Can't be too bad."

"I don't know." A tense look crosses her face. "What's more fun, watching us complete mini challenges or listening to us reveal deep, dark secrets?"

"What if we make a promise not to delve into any of that stuff?" The cameras are rolling, but I'm sure they'll cut this part out. No way they'd want the audience to know we're intentionally botching the game. "Like I won't ask you about your article."

Her lips press into a thin line. "Fine."

My phone buzzes with Nicholas's text. I nod at Trina, who grabs one of the plates the caterers left behind and peels back the wrapping to reveal a plate of bacon. We each grab a slice and she flips over the first card.

Her chewing slows and she reads out loud, "Eat a dried grasshopper." She glances around. "Where am I supposed to get a dried grasshopper?"

I eye the array of plates. "I think they brought us more than food." I lift another cover and sure enough, there's an assortment of silver bags with tiny, white labels. "Here it is." I grab the bag and hold it out to her.

She grimaces. "Truth."

"When you were six, what did you want to be when you grew up?" I ask.

She barely even hesitates. "An astronaut. But then I found out you have to eat all sorts of weird foods out of metal tubes and I changed my mind." She stares pointedly at the bag in my hand.

I laugh and toss it aside, then grab the next card. "Dance the Macarena." I flip the card toward Trina. "Let's do it." I stand, scraping my chair back.

Music fills the room. "Man, this brings back memories." I work my way through the motions while singing along.

Trina puts her hands over her face and laughs. "You look ridiculous."

"Dance with me." I hold out my hand before the next round begins. When she bats it away, I put it behind my head with the other and keep going.

I finish with a flourish, throwing my hands high into the air.

Trina's laughing so hard, she's turning red. Tears stream from her eyes. "I never would've guessed you knew that song, much less the dance."

"You kidding?" I drop back into my seat. "We played that on repeat at my junior high dance. My whole class got in on the action."

She wipes her face and continues chuckling.

I nudge the stack of cards toward her. "A new couch says you won't do the next one." I throw down the challenge like a gauntlet she won't be able to resist.

The spark I'm coming to love lights up her entire face. She snatches the card and flips it over. "Kiss."

A single word has never caused this much indecision in my life. I want to take back what I said, but a challenge is a challenge.

Trina straightens her shoulders, stands, and walks around to my side of the table.

I remain seated, holding my breath for her to slap me or do anything other than kiss me.

Her gaze roams my face, skimming my lips before coming back to my eyes. She moves to stand over me and cups my face in her hands. Her palms are smooth on my morning stubble. Her breath hitches, and her lips touch mine.

Fireworks explode behind my closed eyes. When did I shut them? I reach out for her, my hands finding her hips as though I'm already programmed to know her. I tug her closer. Even with me sitting and her standing, she barely has to bend to reach me. It gives her control of the kiss, and I find I don't mind. Not. At. All. Her fingers sweep into my hair and down to the base of my neck. She curls them there, the points of her nails scraping lightly.

Heaven. I've found heaven, and it's right here in her arms. I never want the moment to end. Our kiss last night was passionate and fierce. This one is tender, almost loving. For a nanosecond, I can almost believe she likes me.

She ends the kiss too soon, but we're both short of breath. My fingers clench of their own accord, like I'm afraid to let her go.

"Guess we're picking out a new couch today." She's absolutely crowing her triumph as she spins away and returns to her seat.

I don't want to play this game anymore. Without meaning to, she's toying with my emotions. I'm taking this more seriously than I should, but I can't help it. I'm starting to have very real feelings for my fake wife.

As we finish the challenge, I do my best to maintain a cheerful smile so we don't lose.

Trina must've noticed something is wrong, because once Nicholas frees us, she grabs my wrist and pulls me toward the bedroom.

Those watching will have a certain idea about what's happening, but I know the truth.

Trina closes the door behind us.

I move to the bed and sink onto the edge. "Plan to yell at me some more?" Good grief, I sound like a wounded pup.

Her feet appear between mine, her painted toes a surprising pop of color. "What's wrong?"

"Nothing." I try to blow the question off. "Not like you want to know."

I hear her gasp but keep my eyes firmly locked onto her pink toenails.

She digs her toes into the carpet. "This is hard on both of us, but if we're going to get through to the end, you need to be honest with me."

"Honest, right." I scoff and look up. "You value honesty, Trina?"

She nods emphatically.

"Is that why you wrote an article claiming I took advantage of a drunk girl? Because you know me and you're so honest?"

Her cheeks turn red and she crosses her arms tight. "I know what I saw."

I meant to do this calmly. Rationally. Well, all that just flew out the window. I've had it up to my eyeballs with dancing around this subject. I wanted Trina to trust me first, but I don't know if that's even possible.

"She's my cousin." I leave out her name in case Trina decides to take the article further instead of deleting it. "She got messed up at a party, and I took her to my house to sober up."

"I don't believe you." She hesitates. "I saw you with her. You...you wrapped your arm around her, and she leaned on you. You both laughed."

"She said something ridiculous about throwing up on my new shoes. They were the first pair of expensive shoes I'd ever bought. I laughed so she wouldn't feel bad when she did throw up."

"You helped her into your car and drove away."

I nod because yes, those are the bare facts of the story. "And she slept all night on my couch, perfectly safe from harm. Because she's family." I sigh, take out my phone, and open an album. "You can look through my pictures. You'll see her in the Christmas photos. Along with my brother and my parents, my aunts and uncles."

She takes the phone from me. "This really matters to you."

"Yes." I can't let her see how much. "That article almost ruined me. Coach put me on suspension and I almost lost my team."

"No wonder you hate me." She blinks rapidly and swipes through the photos. She's a woman on a mission, still trying to find a way to twist this around. "Why wasn't she at our wedding?"

"Not everyone could come at short notice."

"How do I know she isn't your girlfriend in these photos?"

"Geez, you never quit, do you?" I stand and move to the other side of the room. "Just look at her, Trina. She's the spitting image of my mom and the other woman in the room. You've seen pictures of me with my family, you know those are my parents. How much more proof do you need?"

"I'd like to talk to her."

"No." I slash my hands through the air. "Absolutely not. She's been through enough." I hesitate. "And for the record, I don't hate you."

She snorts and hands me back the phone. Remorse lingers in her gaze, and she squeezes my wrist. "I'm sorry. I thought you were a player too."

"Like your last boyfriend." I let out a breath and pinch the back of my neck. "We're not all jerks."

"I'm beginning to see that."

I'm pretty sure I see her changing her mind about me, but it's hard to be sure. We're hidden away in the bedroom where there's no need for either of us to pretend. But it's gotten hard to tell what's real from what's put on for the cameras.

"Can you change the article?" I ask. The hopeful note in my voice makes me sound like a fool, but I'm beyond caring.

Her pinched expression returns. "It's not up to me. My editor decides all that. But I am sorry I followed you, took those pictures, and assumed the worst. It wasn't personal."

"Not for you. But it was very personal to me." I suck in a deep breath and let it out in a rush. "Okay. We have to get out of here. I'm glad we cleared the air."

"Me too." She doesn't seem as nervous anymore. There's even a hint of mischief when she opens the bedroom door. "If you thought that was a challenge, Liam Ashley, just wait until you take me shopping."

I groan dramatically and we walk through the house, pretending once again we're the happiest couple on earth.

Chapter 14

LIAM

I never thought babysitting would be chaotic. I should've known better when the producers announced the next challenge. Especially when they brought Rex in. "Wrecking Ball Rex," the terror of our wedding, zooms into our apartment like a comet and goes straight for the couch.

Nicholas stands in the open door, his face creased in a wide smile. The way he's rubbing his hands together makes me think this guy is more villain than a TV show producer. He cackles when Rex leaps onto the couch and starts jumping. "Alright, folks. Here's your challenge for the night. Show off those parenting skills."

I look to Trina for support, but she's staring at Rex like she's never seen the kid before. "We're in so much trouble."

Well, so much for initiating confidence. Trina's head moves side to side in a slow, methodical shake. "Where are Pam and Dalton?"

Nicholas's smile grows impossibly wide. "We sent them on a date." He holds his finger up. "You are allowed to call them in the case of an emergency, but not for anything else. The challenge ends when we return for Rex."

"You mean my sister let you take her baby boy and cart him over here for a challenge?" Trina's nose scrunches and her hands fist on her hips.

Oh, man. She's mad as a hornet.

If Rex is a wrecking ball, then Trina is a hurricane. She ushers Nicholas from the apartment, waving him off and making goofy faces at the cameras.

Ah, so that's how we're going to play it. I can do that. Surely Rex isn't that bad. I mean, the excitement will wear off soon...right?

Rex jumps from the couch to the coffee table. His sneakers squeak on the glass and he waves his arms to keep his balance. "Whoa, Aunt Trina! Did you see what I did?" He squats. "Watch. I'll do it again."

"No." Trina rushes over and grabs Rex off the table. She sets his feet on the floor and grips his little shoulders. "We're going to have fun tonight, buddy, but you can't jump on everything. Okay?"

Rex shrugs. "Okay." Then he's off again. The kid literally bounces off the walls. He races down the hallway, jumps and kicks his foot against the wall, which sends him careening toward the opposite wall. There go my nice, white walls. Scuff mark city.

I have never seen a kid with this much energy. I shoot Trina a helpless look. She returns it and lifts her hands in an apologetic gesture. "He has diabetes. Not sure if that's the reason for the energy, but he'll slow down eventually." She mutters "I hope," under her breath.

I'm pretty sure she didn't intend for me to hear that part. I lean in close and whisper in her ear, "Nervous breakdown for two, please."

She giggles and pushes me away. More PDA for the cameras. After that little display the other night when she kicked me out of our bedroom, I wasn't sure I could keep this up.

She's worth it, I keep reminding myself.

"Wow." Rex's voice carries from the hallway.

Trina and I shoot worried looks at each other and take off running. I enter the bathroom first.

Rex pokes his head out from the cabinet beneath the sink. He holds up a bottle of cleaner. "This stuff's bad. You should put it up high where I can't reach." He shoves it at Trina.

She takes the bottle and tucks it onto the top shelf of the tiny closet in the hallway.

Only ten minutes have gone by, and I'm more than a little frazzled. "Hey, Rex, why don't we play a game."

Rex's exploration of the space under the sink comes to a freezing halt. He pops out and claps. "I like games. What can we play? Are you any good at hide and seek? I'm the best. Mama never finds me."

Yeah, I don't doubt it. Mama probably tucks herself in the bedroom and hides from little Rexie until he gets bored and comes out on his own. Is it terrible that I'm thinking of doing exactly that? The kid is adorable. Truly.

He's also an exasperating handful. And there's no telling how many hours of this we have left.

"Before we get started, we should check your sugar." Trina holds out her hand toward Rex. "I need to know what you're at before you eat."

Thank goodness she understands all this stuff, because I'm clueless.

He scowls but lets her lead him back to the living room where his dinosaur backpack sits on the floor.

Trina points toward it. "Liam, grab the blue case. It should be in there somewhere. I remember seeing it at the wedding. Pam always puts it in the front zipper pocket."

Rex climbs into Trina's lap and tucks his hands against his stomach. "I want him to do it." He points at me.

I point at me, thumb digging into my chest. "Oh, buddy. You'd better let Aunt Trina. She knows how." I raise an eyebrow, silently asking if I'm telling the truth.

She gives a tiny nod.

Rex kicks his feet, banging his heels into her shins. "No. Aunt Trina holds me and you stick."

My stomach flips like I've ridden a roller coaster a dozen times too many. I don't do blood. Not even a drop. I nearly passed out in the middle of a game once when two players collided and one busted his nose.

Yeah, blood and I don't get along.

Trina rubs a hand over her mouth, no doubt hiding a snicker. She doesn't know about my phobia, but if history is any indication, I just went as pale as Casper the Friendly Ghost.

I unzip the blue container. I understand what the individual pieces are as I've had my finger pricked before. My history with blood tests doesn't make this any easier.

Trina puts the strip in the machine and checks it, then nods at me.

I hold out my hand. It trembles, the fingers quivering hard enough that Rex side-eyes me. He puts his hand on mine, palm up.

I clean the fingertip with alcohol and wait for it to dry and squeeze the lancet tight between my thumb and forefinger.

I can do this. I have to. Trina's watching me. And Rex. All of the people at the network and the hundreds of thousands who will watch the episode when it's aired.

My throat turns dry and there's a sudden roaring in my ears. I know this sound. My vision blurs at the edges and there's a rushing in my head.

Man down. I try to rock back on my heels, but I go too far. My backside smacks the hard floor.

"Wow. He hit hard." Rex leans forward, his eyes wide.

I drop the lancet and use the tail of my shirt to wipe the sweat from my face. "I can't." My hands shake so bad I can barely function.

Trina appears in front of me, her face taking up my entire vision. "Let's go, hot shot." She pulls on my hands and together we manage to move me to the couch.

She lifts my feet onto the arm, then puts pillows under my ankles to raise my feet higher.

Blood rushes to my head and the roaring subsides.

Rex pats my head. "It's okay." He repeats it over and over again. No doubt it's what his mom tells him sometimes.

Or he's worried and doesn't know what else to do. Sweet kid.

Seconds pass, then both Rex and Trina appear on either side of me. Cold and wet slaps my forehead. Trina laughs. "Carefully, Rex."

"Okay." He lifts the cloth, stares at it with a puzzled expression, then swoops it over my eyes. Cold water trickles down my neck, and I bolt upright.

The room spins and I groan.

Trina puts a hand on my chest and pushes me back. I collapse like a sack of bricks.

Rex slaps the cloth over the top of my head and giggles when I try to roll away.

I lose track of time as I lay there letting Trina and Rex take care of me. Though "care," is subjective.

Rex continues to drown me in cold water, but I have to admit it's helping.

When I can finally sit up, Trina pats my shoulder. "That...was not what I expected."

"Yeah, well." I shrug. "I don't like blood."

"Obviously." She laughs, tries to hide it, then caves and roars with absolute glee. "You went down like a tree." She slams her palm into the couch. "One minute up, the next *wham*. Never seen anything like it."

"Happy to give you something to laugh at," I grumble but the sour mood doesn't last long. It's nice to see her smile and laugh, even if it is at my expense. "You don't think we'll lose the challenge because of that, do you?"

"Nah." She shakes her head and pushes to standing. "You keep an eye on Rex. I'll fix something to eat."

"Trade!" I jump up and race for the kitchen, patting her shoulder as I pass. "Tag, you're it."

"Tag? I love tag." Rex screeches back into the room so fast I'm surprised there isn't smoke rolling out from under his heels. He spins around and around. "Aunt Trina, catch me."

She glares at me.

I grin and wiggle my fingers at her. "Better run, Auntie, before he finds something else dangerous."

Her eyes widen, and she bolts after the little terror.

I take a second in the kitchen to compose myself. Kids. I never decided if I wanted them or not. Rex is a handful, but he's growing on me. We'll see if the apartment is standing when the challenge is over.

I'm not a complete imbecile in the kitchen, but I've no idea what to fix a kid Rex's age. He's like, four? Five? I never asked. Sheesh. Some uncle I am.

I opt for my favorite: Mac 'n cheese. What kid doesn't like a good, carb-filled meal.

"Liam?" The fear in Trina's voice jolts through me. "Something's wrong with Rex."

I drop the box on the counter and race down the hallway where I heard her voice.

She sits in the middle of the bedroom floor, Rex in her arms. Fear fills her eyes. "His insulin levels may be off."

"But we—you—just checked." I spin around, searching like the answer might be right behind me.

She groans and pats Rex's pale cheek. "I did, but Pam said this happens sometimes. She mentioned he still crashes."

"Crashes? What does that mean?"

"I don't know." Panic flares in her eyes. "We have to do something."

I snatch my phone out and call Clay.

Thankfully, he answers right away. "Hey, bro. Things getting exciting yet?"

"You could say that." I pace in front of Trina. "We're babysitting tonight and something's wrong with him."

"Symptoms?" Clay barks.

I pass the phone to Trina. "It's my brother. He's a pediatric surgeon. Man saves kids' lives for a living. Tell him what's wrong."

Trina rattles off Rex's symptoms while I consider scooping Rex up and hauling him to the nearest hospital.

"Jelly beans?" Trina's voice raises an octave. She shakes her head and passes the phone back to me. "He says to give him jelly beans."

"I don't have jelly beans," I practically scream into the phone. "Where am I supposed to get jelly beans at this time of night?"

"Take it easy. All diabetics know to carry sugary foods around for a quick pick me up in times like this." Clay's calm voice is the only thing keeping me sane right now.

Rex groans and his head lolls to the side.

Trina pats his cheeks. "Rex? Rex?"

"Don't feel good." Rex's eyes flutter open.

Clay speaks again, and I grip the phone harder. "Check his bag for anything sugary. Candy bars. Glucose tabs. Anything. I'll be there in ten minutes."

I run from the room, bouncing off the walls like Rex when he first arrived, and grab his bag from the living room. Jelly beans. Jelly beans. I paw through the contents, crowing with triumph when I discover a plastic bag of candy.

"Did you find something?" Trina steps out from the hallway, Rex in her arms.

I hurry over and hold out my arms. "I'll hold him. See if you can get him to eat."

She takes a piece of candy from the bag while I prop Rex up. "Come on, Rex. It's a red one. Your favorite."

He opens his mouth and Trina pops the candy inside. We're both silent, listening to him chew and swallow. He opens again, and she gives him another candy.

With each one, he becomes more alert, his complexion brightens, and the light comes back into his eyes.

"Whew," I say with a chuckle. "Good thing we didn't panic."

She rolls her eyes and gives Rex the last candy.

The front door bangs open and Clay rushes inside. He examines Rex without ever moving the kid from my arms.

All of a sudden, I don't want to let the kid go.

Nicholas comes in several minutes later. He's not smiling this time. It's the most somber expression I've ever seen on the guy.

It sends a nervous tingling through my fingers like I get before every game. I know from the wrinkle between his eyes what he's about to say.

Trina's head bows forward in defeat.

"Sorry, guys." Nicholas pats each of us on the shoulder. "Better luck next time." Once he hears from Clay that Rex is fine, his smile slowly reappears. "So, this one was a bust. You guys were doing great for a while, but you panicked. We have to call that a loss. You'll be given a punishment within the next few days."

"I don't feel like we lost." I tighten my grip on Rex, who's currently trying to climb me like a monkey. I give in and let him scramble onto my back. He swings his legs around my neck and wraps his arms around my head.

Nicholas spreads his hands out. "The decision has been made."

I take Trina's hand and squeeze. "That's not what I mean. Sure, we lost the challenge, but this has been one of the most fun nights I've ever had."

Trina nods. "Bring on the consequences. Whatever it is, we'll face it." She smiles up at me. "Together."

Rex squeezes his arms together, smooshing my face.

Trina, Clay, and Nicholas laugh.

I would, but I'm too busy wondering if our kids would be anything like Rex. I think I'd like that.

Chapter 15

"Watching parenting videos isn't that bad." I place the last of the snacks on the coffee table and settle next to Liam.

"Three hours followed by a test. You don't call that bad? I hope you're the one taking notes." Liam leans forward and scoops a handful of chips. His hand is so large, he's removed a third of the bowl's contents.

I take half his chips. "It's 50/50 in this relationship. You must stay awake the whole time. You snooze, you lose."

"Babe, I'm being honest here. My desire to study is like my relationship with kale—we just don't get along."

I cover my mouth as I talk around the chips. "You'll be fine. The first video is Super Nanny. She's hilarious. I love her English accent. 'That's unacceptable, Tommy.'"

"Never heard of her."

"It's an old series. I only watched a couple of episodes, but I remember how crazy the kids were. By the end, she'd have them cleaning the house."

Liam leans in and whispers. "Reality TV—it's not what it seems." He kisses my cheek and sits upright. "Let's do this. I can't wait to try these techniques on 'Wrecking Ball Rex.'"

I click play on the remote. "That's the spirit." But I doubt even Super Nanny's methods could settle Rex's antics.

The first hour zooms by, but Liam hardly sits still. If the guy would concentrate on the videos like he does performing for the cameras, leaning all over me, we would have this test in the basket. At one point, he places a pillow on my lap and asks me to stroke his hair. I tell him in my best British accent that his behavior is unacceptable.

The second video isn't so entertaining. It's more of a documentary and even I'm bored as heck.

Liam wraps his arms around me and snuggles. "Save me from going into a coma." He tucks some hair behind my ear. "I know a way to make the night more interesting." He nibbles on my earlobe.

I inch away, giggling. He knows my ticklish spot. "I'll send you to the naughty mat for time out." I point at the TV. "Focus."

He holds up his forefinger. "One kiss." He wriggles his eyebrows before leaning in, and whispers, "for the ratings, Trina."

He's using my competitive nature to his advantage. I want to steal votes from the other couples. Liam is right. We do need to keep up the PDA. One kiss won't hurt.

"Fine." I huff like it's the most annoying thing on the planet to kiss a gorgeous basketball player.

His arm drapes around my shoulder. Liam twirls my hair as he brushes his lips against mine.

Melting at his caress, I tug on his shirt and pull him closer.

Liam takes his time, drawing out the kiss. It's like he wants it to last as long as possible. Just as I've come to the conclusion he's still acting, I sense a shadow. With his free hand, he's grabbed a nearby pillow, and is strategically placing it to shield our faces from the cameras. His kiss becomes passionate, taking us way out-of-bounds.

What is he doing? Panic surges within me. He's breaking our unspoken rule, the one where we pretend we don't enjoy PDA.

No. No. No. This can't happen. I should call "foul."

For two seconds more, I pretend I'm unaware of the pillow and allow him to kiss me. My lips soften, melding with his. Mmm. I could kiss this man for hours.

I open my eyes, as if I'm only just realizing the cameras can't see. "Liam," I whisper, my voice filled with longing.

He continues his assault on my senses, his lips now trailing along my jawline. His response is muffled against my skin, breathless, yet on a mission. "Yeah?"

"What're you doing?" My voice trembles.

He pulls back slightly, a mischievous glint in his eyes. "Kissing my wife, like a good husband should."

I shake my head, a silent protest.

"Fine," he concedes, dropping the pillow with a playful thud. His hands find their place, cradling my face with tenderness. And with a renewed sense of determination, he continues to kiss me, but this time, slower and more deliberate, as if savoring every moment, every stolen breath.

The kiss has gone on long enough. I pull away from him. "Okay. You got your *one* kiss." I emphasize the word, 'one'.

He smiles dreamily at me before grabbing the pillow. He places his head on my lap again.

I resist rolling my eyes. He's so cheeky tonight. What's gotten into him?

The last video drags on, and Liam falls asleep. I find myself stroking his hair like I would to a Persian cat. Thank goodness he's softly snoring.

I give him a gentle shake. "Wake up. We've got to do the test."

The first question pops onto the screen, offering multiple choice answers. How many questions are there? And what if we don't pass again? Do we earn another consequence? Get sent to the naughty mat?

Liam rises from the dead and rubs his eyes. "What did I miss?"

"Not much—mostly how to toddler-proof a home. I'll help with those final questions."

I wave the remote at the screen and read the first one aloud.

"You found your toddler drawing on the wall. How do you respond?

A) Give them a high-five and tell them they have amazing artistic talent.

B) Laugh it off and say, 'Oops! Let's save the walls for paper, okay?' and help them clean the wall.

C) Raise your voice and send them straight to timeout.

D) Start crying and wonder where you went wrong as a parent."

Liam snickers. "I'd say A."

I roll my eyes and click on B.

A large green check mark flashes, then the next question appears.

You're in a shopping mall when your toddler throws a tantrum. How do you handle the situation?

A) Join them in the tantrum, hoping to outdo their performance and embarrass your toddler so they stop.

B) Give in to their demands and buy them anything they want to calm them quickly.

C) Scoop them up and find a quiet corner or a less crowded area to help them calm down and address their needs.

D) Ignore the tantrum completely and continue shopping as if nothing is happening.

"My mom probably would've picked D," Liam says. "These questions are too easy. We're going to ace this. Go for C."

I select C and we get it right. But the next question isn't as simple.

Your child refuses to eat their vegetables at dinner. How do you handle the situation?

A) Insist that they finish all the vegetables on their plate, using gentle encouragement and positive reinforcement.

B) Respect their decision and offer alternative healthy food options that they enjoy, ensuring they still receive proper nutrition.

C) Threaten to take away their favorite toy or activity if they don't eat their vegetables.

D) Let them skip the vegetables altogether and indulge in their favorite dessert.

Liam and I debate over A or B for five minutes then finally select A.

A green check mark flashes on the screen and a message appears below:

In this question, both options A and B can be considered appropriate depending on the parent's approach and the specific circumstances. It's important to consider the child's individual preferences and overall nutritional balance when addressing mealtime challenges.

We continue to go through the questions, but they get more difficult. When we think two might be correct, we pick the wrong one. Don't tell me this is rigged to fail as well?

By the end of the test, our score flashes on the TV.

58%

Liam high-fives me before giving me a firm side hug. "We can babysit Wrecking Ball Rex again and there's a 58% chance we'll survive."

I kiss his cheek and thread my fingers through his hair. "Let's both sleep on the couch tonight." This is the safer option after the way he kissed me earlier. It wouldn't make sense to the viewers if Liam was sent to the couch again.

His eyes light up like a kid having his best friend stay for a sleepover. "I'll be the dessert spoon, and you be the teaspoon."

"What?"

He takes the remote from me, clicks off the TV, and slides it to the coffee table. After dimming the lights, Liam slips in behind me and pulls me into a position where I'm lying on my side. His leg tangles with mine, and I nestle into his cozy embrace.

With his other hand, he tugs the throw blanket over us, and settles his arm around my waist. A soft sigh escapes his lips, causing a tingling sensation on the nape of my neck. Did I make the right choice? This is all too real now. How can I continue pretending that I'm not falling for him?

Chapter 16

LIAM

I knock on the door of the apartment the producers specified and gaze at my beautiful wife. "That new sectional is great. I don't remember the last time I slept so well on anything that wasn't my own bed. I'm glad you chose it."

Trina grins and nods toward the door. "Ready for this?" She sweeps her hair over her shoulder and twists a strand around her finger. Then she drops her hair and clasps her hands.

I thread our fingers together and brush my thumb over her knuckles. "Am I ready to crush the competition? You bet."

She lifts her chin. "Right. This should be easy. It's multiple choice."

I work to keep the tension from my body. "Wait, what's your favorite color? I bet that's one of the questions."

The door opens before she answers, and a couple greets us with enthusiastic hugs. "Welcome, welcome." The woman waves us inside. "Come on in. You're the last ones to show up."

Trina shoots me the death glare—aka the wife stare. She wanted to leave earlier, but I didn't see the point. We're not here to make friends.

I'm second-guessing my choice as we walk in and laughter rings out from the living room where two other newlywed couples from the show occupy a massive leather couch. Okay, I might have been wrong. Will Trina punish me? At least the new couch is comfortable.

"Okay," the man who opened the door claps his hands. "Introductions." He motions for those sitting to stand. "We'll go around the room. I'm Matt, and this is my wife, Deborah." He squeezes her to his side, and she smiles up at him like he set the moon in the sky.

Trina watches them with narrowed eyes, assessing the competition.

The couple on the left end of the couch stands almost a foot apart. "I'm Regina. This is Victor." She jabs her thumb at him, and he scowls. Okay, so they probably don't know anything about each other.

Since this competition is about who can correctly answer the most questions about their partner, I strike them off my list as potential competitors.

The last couple are hard to figure out. They stand close together but without touching. Honestly, they appear a lot like me and Trina. A bit uncomfortable but willing to give it a shot.

"William," the man says.

The woman nods. "Alyssa."

Trina introduces us, and Matt rubs his hands together the way Nicholas does.

Trina's eyes narrow further. Coincidence or something else?

"Everyone take a seat." Deborah ushers us to the couch. "Now that we're all here, we can relay the rules." She snatches the TV remote. "So, here's what happens. At exactly seven o'clock, a question will appear on the screen. We all have cards labeled A, B, C, or D. Choose the card you think your spouse would choose. It should be obvious if the question specifies the husband or the wife."

The TV brightens. "It will look like this," Matt points at the blue screen.

Across the top in bold letters, I read: Which is your wife's favorite?

    A) A long soak in the tub
    B) A night of stargazing
    C) Being left alone with a good book
    D) Ice cream and board games

"Now," says Deborah, "you'll each choose your answers without looking at or speaking to each other. The timer will count down, and when the buzzer sounds, everyone reveals their answers." She lifts her eyebrows. "Any questions?"

A mixture of tension and fun mingles in the air. I reach for a handful of chips from one of the bowls in the center of the coffee table. "Sounds easy." I'm nowhere near as confident as I sound. If all the questions are like the sample, then I'm sunk.

Trina leans back and settles her cards in her lap. "Which one would you pick for me?"

"C," I answer without hesitation.

She grins and smacks the card against the back of my arm.

A countdown clock appears on the TV screen. Trina straightens.

Matt and Deborah fall over each other laughing as they make their way over to the last chair. Matt sits and pulls Deborah into his lap. They snuggle into each other.

I glance at Trina and roll my eyes.

She puts a hand over her mouth to hide her giggle.

The TV screen flashes, and a question pops up.

What is your husband's favorite color?

A) Blue
B) Purple
C) Red
D) Yellow

What if someone has a color that isn't listed? I scramble to flip to the card I need and hold it tight to my chest.

The others do the same.

The screen changes, counting down.

3

2

1

Reveal!

We all flip our cards around. Both Trina and I have chosen A.

Matt and Deborah are on C.

The other two couples chose differing answers, so the point comes down between us and the lovey-dovey couple.

"How do we know if we're right?" Trina seems delighted to have picked the same answer as me. "You wear blue shirts a lot. I figured it was your favorite."

I kiss her cheek.

"Trina and Deborah are correct." A voice booms from the TV.

"Whoa." I slap a hand to my chest. "Nicholas?"

His laughter sounds distorted. "Cool, huh? A quick note Deborah forgot to mention. We have pre-recorded answers based on information sheets you all filled out before you married. If you've forgotten what you answered then and you choose something different now, it will be taken into consideration if you and your spouse still choose the right answer."

"Good to know," Trina mutters from the side of her mouth.

"The winner tonight will be treated to a romantic dinner at Paulo's, the luxurious restaurant known for its flame-seared steak. Now, prepare for the next question." Nicholas's voice disappears and the screen changes again.

The next thirty minutes pass in a flurry of laughter...except for Regina and Victor, who don't get any questions right.

I get three right in a row, and my confidence soars. Trina and I make a pretty good team. I might not have ever asked her these questions, but I've come to understand her these last few weeks.

She gets one wrong about me, some random question about my favorite thing to sleep in. It's shorts, but no doubt she chose the shirt and shorts option because that's what I've been sleeping in since she moved in.

"I was trying to make you more comfortable," I whisper in her ear. "Especially since you showed up in flannel pajamas for our wedding night."

Her cheeks turn pink, and she hides behind her cards.

All of a sudden, we're tied with Matt and Deborah, and a rapid-fire round begins. The competition is fierce, but Trina and I manage to yank the victory out from under their noses.

We leap to our feet and cheer, hugging and jumping around.

The look on Victor's face puts a damper on my enthusiasm, but it's got nothing to do with us. He and Regina have been arguing off and on all night.

"Whew." Deborah fans herself with her cards. "That was fun." She stands. "Any of you ladies care to join me for some female talk?"

Regina leaps to her feet. "Count me in."

Alyssa follows at a slower pace, but soon all the women have gathered in one corner of the room, leaving us men in the middle. An uncomfortable silence settles.

Matt clears his throat. "Anyone up for some basketball?" He grabs the remote. "Liam, I think I have one of your games recorded."

"Oh no. Please don't indulge him," Trina calls out from across the room. "Make him watch an opposing team."

The men chuckle, and soon Matt has a game going. I don't mind. It gives me a chance to study and gather intel on other teams we might compete with.

Trina's head is bent toward the other women. They seem to be having a wonderful time. I'm glad. Maybe it will help her get through the rest of our time together. It's rapidly coming to a close. I try to ignore the pang in my chest at the idea of never seeing her again. It's for the best, but it's not what I want.

TRINA

I lean over the island counter, swirl my juice, then take a sip. "Deb, I love the beach art on the walls. Was this originally your place or Matt's?"

She flashes a smile. "Matt's, but as soon as I moved in, we redecorated." She points to the shells lining a white-washed shelf. "They're from my house. Matt wanted me to bring some of the themes I had going so this would feel more like home."

"It looks great," I say.

Regina crosses her arms. "I wish Victor was thoughtful."

I'm so going to write an article about Victor and Regina, but Melanie already told me they're at the bottom of the ladder. But where is couple number five? Time for some investigation.

"Hey, Deb. Was anyone not able to make it tonight?"

She leans over the island, and the other ladies mimic her. "Apparently, they've dropped out. The producers haven't released the episode yet, but Shona and Jayden had a big blow up. They can't stand each other." She places a finger to her lips. "But you didn't hear it from me. I asked about them since I was hosting, and Nicholas told me."

I straighten. My boss is going to be so pleased. We can leak this gossip days before the show airs. But I need more info about these ladies too.

I face Alyssa. "Do you think you'll last the full three months?"

Alyssa's cheeks flush pink. My tact isn't great. I've built no report with her and just reached for the jugular vein.

"I mean . . ." I offer a small smile. "You seem like me—a little uncomfortable about this whole ordeal." I wave a hand down. "Which I totally get."

Her smile brightens, like she's grateful for the connection. Alyssa gently touches her throat, her voice filled with vulnerability. "It's the strangest experience, isn't it? It feels like being caught in some bizarre version of the Truman Show. How are we supposed to genuinely fall in love when we virtually have no privacy? I find it hard to be myself and relax."

My fingers skim Alyssa's shoulder in a comforting gesture. "Exactly. I feel the same way." My hand naturally falls back to my side. "But you know what? As time goes on, I find myself getting more comfortable in front of the cameras. I even look forward to the journal videos."

Alyssa frowns like she's chewing on sour candy. "That's the worst part for me."

Regina tosses her hair over her shoulder. "The journal booth is my favorite spot in the house. Sometimes I hide there until Victor comes looking for me."

Gee. Things are that bad. Maybe their make-shift booth isn't a half-bath.

I gesture to the ladies to come in nice and close like I'm going to reveal a big secret. Three pairs of eyes stare at me in anticipation.

"Have any of you had any major things go wrong in the challenges? For instance, we had a water relay and my jet ski failed. We didn't beat the timer."

Regina's face flashes murder. "Yes!"

I glance over to the guys, and Liam sends me a concerned look. Victor rolls his eyes and waves the men's attention back to the TV.

I whisper to Regina. "What happened?"

She leans toward me, mirroring my secretive posture. "Well," her voice is barely audible. "The first incident was minor. We had a cooking challenge, and I swear, someone replaced the sugar with salt." She shakes her head, her eyes reflecting exasperation. "Victor thinks I'm hopeless at baking and didn't hide his disappointment. But I'm glad to see that side of him early on." She lifts a palm. "Like who cares if I can't bake? Store muffins are cheaper than the ingredients to make them."

I nod, a smile tugging at my lips.

"The next weird thing that happened," Regina's tone drops, "was during a team-building exercise. They blindfolded me and put me in a maze and gave me a walkie-talkie. Victor stood in the lookout tower and instructed me on how to get out." Her eyes go wild, and her voice rises in volume. "Well, coincidentally, the walkie-talkies kept fading out. I was stuck in that maze for fifty-minutes. Victor and I were yelling at each other by the end, and I nearly collapsed in a heap of tears. It was awful."

I wrap an arm around Regina. "That is awful. And I thought we had it bad. No wonder you want to tear each other's hair out."

She looks up at me. "Is it that obvious? I can't stand my husband. Can't wait for this show to be over."

I rub her shoulder. "Maybe once the pressure is off, you two can really discover each other. It might end up working out okay."

Her brows shoot up. "You think so?"

"You're married now. Might as well give it your best shot." Gee, I'm such a hypocrite.

"Do you think you and Liam will end up staying together?" Her question is genuine and it's a fair one to ask.

Flutters rise in my chest. What would it be like to have a future with Liam? I swallow hard. "I hope we do."

Chapter 17

LIAM

This can't be real. I read the article again. It's worse than I thought. The words skating past my eyes turns my skin clammy and cold.

In a world where nothing is as it seems, Reality TV brings us a whole new level of unrealistic expectations. When two strangers are married and thrown together to sink or swim within three months, you would think the show entertaining enough. But that's just the tip of the iceberg. Weekly challenges await the participants, and some teams will draw blood to achieve victory. While "Bride at First Sight" is geared toward the idea that arranged marriages can work in today's society, there's an undeniable reality that watching these couples scrap it out will garner untold attention. The truth is, Liam and Trina are a joke. If you don't believe me, ask Trina herself. Her exact words were, "Liam follows me around like a little lovesick puppy dog." I'm not sure how much more I can take.

I couldn't be more winded if I'd been gut-punched. Nothing about the article itself is out of the ordinary, but the last part is vicious.

I saw Trina typing something similar yesterday. She didn't see me watching her from the bedroom door, but I caught snippets of the article from across the room.

I don't mind the article. It's actually pretty good, considering what we've gone through. What bothers me is the line at the bottom.

"While these couples are forced to eke out victories while answering multiple choice questions about their partners, what challenges really await them?"

That line unsettles me. That episode shouldn't have aired yet. The release schedule is a week behind actual events. It means Trina has been sending stuff about the show—about us—to the newspaper.

The phone screen flickers, and Coach's name pops up. I answer with a grunt.

"Got a problem, Ashley." His voice is gruff and no nonsense. Nothing unusual, but a bubble of doubt clenches in my gut.

"What's that?" I scrub a hand over my cheek and try to rein in my temper. It doesn't often get the best of me like it did the other night when I told Trina the truth about Lindsay, but it's threatening to boil over now.

Papers rustle in the background. "Seems she's been spilling her guts. About you. The team. And this whole marriage experience."

I wince and press my thumb and forefinger into my eyes. "It's not that bad, Coach." Even now, I want to believe the best about Trina.

"Liam." Coach's chair squeaks. I can't remember the last time he used my first name. "You need to pull your head out of the sand, son. Run a search on your name. Articles are surfacing all over the place. And none of them are flattering."

"What? No. That can't be true." My pulse kicks into overdrive. I pull the phone from my ear and tap over to a search engine. A few clicks, and my name is in the search bar. The burst of anger spills over as my name appears alongside multiple ridiculous headlines.

"Ashley, the jock who knew better."

"Liam Ashley, America's Bitter Bachelor."

"Ashley Wedding Hoax. Reporter gets the inside scoop on Liam's personal life."

They're all by the same person. M.J. Albert. I don't recognize the name.

I suck in a breath and click the last one.

It reads like a documentary of our time together. Things I never wanted exposed to the world are right there. But Trina's getting roasted too. The media storm has pinned each of us with a firestorm of labels and accusations.

Many of them accuse Trina of paying me to choose her so she could get the article of her career.

I skim the details until I reach the middle and then stop to read.

"This new article marks the first time Trina Smith has reported on the illustrious Liam Ashley in a year. Her first article, under Kat Smith—showcased here—tells of a very different side to the congenial basketball player. Her article portrays him as a player, both on and off the court. And it seems her opinion hasn't changed much during this 'marriage.'"

"Your wife has been outed as an undercover journalist." Coach's voice brings me back. Barely. "She's been using you this whole time."

"Trina hasn't been reporting since we were married." I rub a hand over my forehead. I'm sick of being the media's punching bag.

"Trina *is* M.J. Albert. She's been putting out those articles every week, giving tidbits of information." Coach sighs. "Someone figured it out. Hacked her computer maybe, but her boss confirmed it. Trina's planning an exclusive on the whole experience of being your wife."

"No." I can't stand the thought of Trina doing this to me.

Coach blows out a breath. "I'm sorry, son. Do what you gotta do, but I need you at practice."

"You know this for a fact? It's not a rumor from another reporter?" I need confirmation before I'll believe. I've never liked going off gut feelings or another person's opinion. I need facts.

"I spoke to her boss myself. When this all started at three in the morning, I called him. He verified the information."

"Okay." It's all I can say. Anything else takes too much effort.

"I really am sorry."

"Yeah," I sigh. "Me too." I hang up and take stock of what I need to do next.

Practice? When my whole life is falling apart like a line of badly stacked dominos? My stomach churns. How could I have been so blind? All those sweet moments we shared, the stolen kisses, the late-night talks—they were all part of her plan to make me look bad. I should've known she was just using me, just like she did in her first article.

I clench my fists, anger boiling inside. She's been out to get me from the start, and I fell right into her trap. I've been so stupid. I knew I'd never find true love through the show, not when all those women were attracted to my money and fame.

I shoot off a message to Cool. I made a mistake, choosing Trina.

She's no different from all the others. She found a way to use me. I should've known changing her mind was a pointless exercise the night I told her the truth about Lindsay.

The bedroom door opens, and Trina's light steps whisper down the hallway. I continue scrolling on my phone. Videos pop up like gophers. They're everywhere.

Most are about Trina being a reporter. They're calling her the "Undercover Lover."

"Hey." Her voice is sweet and soft. She stands in the center of the room, looking almost uncertain. "When can we go shopping for my finale dress? We should color coordinate."

I freeze in place, body ice cold. "We won't be going anywhere." I spin the phone around to let her see. "We won't be doing anything together anymore."

She reaches for my phone, but I snatch it back. "I don't understand."

"I do now." I stand and pace back and forth across the kitchen floor. "I should've known. You were looking for a story that night. Why else would you be there?"

Trina grabs her phone and types. Her face pales.

"No wonder you didn't fight any harder when I chose you. I'd just handed you your career on a platter." I tunnel both hands through my hair and continue pacing. Standing still is unbearable.

"I didn't do this." She waves at the phone. "It wasn't me."

"No?" I ask with a caustic laugh. "Excuse me for not believing you. Not when you refused to admit the truth about my cousin. Or even wrote the article in the first place."

I head toward the front door. I can't do this. The cameras watch our every move, they hear our every word. The last thing I want is more attention. And Trina's can of worms will bring its own crazy frenzy, even without the goodies the show producers reveal later.

"Liam, wait." Trina follows me.

"I need you to be gone by the time I get back from practice." I grab my gym bag and heave it over my shoulder.

Are those tears on Trina's lashes? I yank the front door open and storm out. Stupid wishful thinking. Trina doesn't care about me.

She tried to tell me. Over and over again.

All those kisses. My cheeks burn. Though she kissed me like she might love me—not real.

I tug a baseball cap low over my forehead and tuck my chin against my chest. The media isn't always lying in wait for me, but I've learned to err on the side of caution. I sneak around the corner and dart to the back of the building.

Shameless reporters cluster around my car.

Cool pulls up as I'm jogging across the parking lot, weaving between cars. He throws a hand out the window and waves for me to hurry. I kick into a run and dive into his car at the same time the reporters roar. They've caught sight of me.

Cool punches the gas. The Camaro's engine revs, and the tires squeal. We shoot out into the road fast enough that I hang onto the door while trying to click the seatbelt and shove my bag into the floorboard.

"Thanks." I finally get the belt to click and relax my death grip on the door.

Cool shoots me a smile. "I said we'd be there for you. Didn't expect to get to pull out my Fast and Furious moves though." He pats the steering wheel. "Always wanted to have a reason to do that."

I ease my head back against the headrest and remove the ball cap.

"You want to talk about it?" Cool asks. He glances at me every now and then, his expression curious but not demanding anything from me.

I shake my head. "Nah, man. I'm good."

"Yeah. Well, we'll see about that. Coach said you might not be at practice today." Cool grimaces. "We're supposed to run today. Getting too slow out there. No footwork. And with our game against the Morgans coming up, we gotta get some speed going."

"Right now, I got enough anger to keep me running for hours."

Cool pulls into the gym parking lot.

Cameras flash, and two dozen people race for the car. Security swarms out from the building and works to corral the reporters.

One gets too close to the car for Cool's comfort. He revs the engine again and lets it jump forward, coming closer to the guy trying to see through the tinted windows. "Guess they called their buddies. Told them to look for my car."

"Guess so," I say as I slump down. "Sorry."

"It's all good." Cool smacks my leg.

We sit back and wait for security to do their job. The rumble of the engine soothes me in a weird way. I'll be okay eventually. Right now I'm a mess of confused emotions.

I thought Trina and I were making progress. Heck, I was halfway in love with her. The puppy dog comment lodges in the back of my throat and steals my breath.

How did I not see this coming? She's been out to get me since that first article. Am I so unlovable I'll never find anyone? I hate to be dramatic, but seriously. When will it be my turn to fall in love and have someone love me?

Never. I scoff at the idea of putting myself out there again. There's no need. I tried twice, and I crashed and burned twice.

There is no third times a charm for me, because I'm done. I'd resigned myself to the life of a bachelor because the women I meet are all after my money and fame. I expected Trina to be different. And she was. She wanted me for an entirely different reason. "Bride at First Sight" was supposed to be a way to get past those with ulterior motives.

The security guards wave us forward. Cool pulls into his parking spot and kills the engine. We sit there a few seconds, the silence thick with what I'm holding in.

I grab my bag and hop out, Cool on my heels. Security forms a barricade around us. The reporters are corralled off in the grass far away, but they're still taking pictures and shouting questions.

"Liam, where's Trina?"

"Did you know about her all along?"

"Are you going to continue the show?"

I tune them out as best I can. Cool's expression is one I've only seen a couple times before. He usually plays it up for the reporters, but when they get out of line, like they are now, he turns into a beast.

He moves to block the reporters from getting a good shot of me.

It won't help. They'll post some blurry image and make it look like I needed Cool's help or something ridiculous. By the end of the day, there will be a hundred more articles. I'll be accused of everything from alcoholism and drug abuse to worse things. Things I endured before, thanks to Trina.

Thinking of her makes my stomach twist. Will she leave like I said, or will I go home and find her there, waiting for me?

I never want to see her again.

Chapter 18

TRINA

After bawling my eyes out and shoving my belongings into suitcases, I have my ah-ha moment.

I stomp my way to one of the ceiling cameras and shake a finger. "No way. This. Is. Not. How. It. Ends."

I leave my packed bags, grab my purse, and brace for the collateral damage. It's time to clean up my mess.

As soon as I step into the undercover parking lot, a swarm of reporters charge at me like soccer players. I slip my sunglasses over my eyes and hold up my palm, signaling "stop." I'm no longer intimidated by cameras and microphones. It's been my life for the last few months.

Questions bombard me left and right. I spot the microphone badge I want to see. CNN.

I point to that reporter and shout over the noise. "You. Exclusive interview. Now. Let's go."

I push through the sea of photographers, and Alecia from CNN leads me to a BMW. Large cash offers chase us, but I'm not doing this for money. I'm going big or going home.

The twenty minutes to the city race by as Alecia fangirls me. She can't believe her luck. Her cameraman sits in the backseat, gazing at the passing cars.

We find a quiet spot downtown at a public park. Alecia orders two lattes at a coffee van, and we sit at a picnic bench. "We'll go for the heart-to-heart interview style, like we're friends sharing over coffee."

I tilt my head and shrug one shoulder. "Whatever works. Will this air tonight?"

Alecia taps her lips. "I can't promise anything, but they might slip it into this evening's news." She lifts her cell. "Give me a minute. With the blow up in the media this morning, our producer will want to prioritize an exclusive."

She makes a call, excitement in her tone. After she ends the conversation, she turns to me, eyes bright. "Daryl wants to speak with you. He's meeting us here."

"Daryl?"

"The production manager."

"Okay. I have no other plans." I chuckle, but it's a self-deprecating laugh. My life is in no-man's land now. Where am I going to live? I leased out my apartment for three months. The tenants have two weeks left. I don't want to go back to my job after what Mike did to my M.J. Albert articles. The show has refused to pay me for breaching the contract, and they will definitely cut me off after this interview. I don't care. All I care about is vindicating Liam.

Alecia rubs her hands together. "Ready?"

I nod and the cameraman signals from behind the camera.

Alicia beams perfect white teeth toward the lens. "Tonight, we have an exclusive interview with Trina Smith from the reality TV show, 'Bride at First Sight.' Trina has agreed to open up about her controversial articles and the truth behind the headlines. I'm Alicia Nickols, CNN news." She faces me, holding the mic under her chin. "Trina, or should I call you M.J. Albert? There's been a lot of speculation surrounding your articles. Can you shed some light on this?"

This is it, my chance to set the record straight about Liam. I take a deep breath and straighten my posture, meeting Alicia's gaze with unwavering determination. "Absolutely, Alicia. First and foremost, I want to clarify that I did indeed write those articles under the pen name M.J. Albert. However, there is a crucial detail the public is unaware of—the final article that was published was not my original work."

Alicia leans in, her eyes widening. "Are you saying someone tampered with your articles? Can you elaborate?"

I nod, the revelation heavy on my shoulders. "Yes, I'd love to. It's standard procedure to have an editor review and polish article drafts. Unfortunately, my editors took it upon themselves to make significant changes without my consent. They altered the tone and content in a way that portrayed Liam Ashley in a negative light, deviating from my original intention."

Alicia's brows furrow. "That's concerning. Why do you think the editor made those amendments without informing you?"

I take a moment to gather my thoughts. In my industry, it's a huge no-no to slam a publication you've worked for. I'll basically flush my entire career down the toilet. In fact, by doing this exclusive, I've already ruined any chance of remaining employed with them.

"I believe it was a combination of factors. Liam and I had a history, and there was some unresolved tension between us. My boss knew I didn't want to be a contestant. The editors can never resist the opportunity for a sensational story and exploited our complicated relationship for maximum impact. I wasn't available for back-and-forth communication due to the demands of the show, so my boss would have approved the edits on my behalf."

Alicia pulls the microphone under her chin, a frown creasing her brow. "Let's back up a moment. You said you didn't want to be on the show? How do you and Liam share a history? Did you date him in the past?"

I shake my head. There's no going back now. I need to tell them everything, no matter how poorly it reflects on my character. If my heart bleeds on national TV, so be it. "I wrote an article for MA Times about Liam a year ago under the name Kat Smith. I thought I saw him take a girl home but was mistaken." I hold up a hand. "I'll get to that bit in a minute."

I take another breath. "I attended the opening night of 'Bride at First Sight' as a sports journalist. I had removed my media tag. Then Liam spotted me and took a chance to prove how wrong I was about him. How he's actually a decent guy who didn't deserve to be smeared by my wrong assumptions."

"Wow. But you went along with his selection. Why? That's a huge commitment." She laughs.

"I was put on the spot and did my best to get out of the situation, but my boss ultimately talked me into it. I promised Liam I would make him pay for choosing me on live national TV."

"How did Liam respond to your threat?"

"He laughed. Uncontrollably." I smirk at the memory of him huddled in the corner of the limousine, hands clutched to his stomach. "You see, he knew there was no dirt to find. The woman he took home that night was a close family friend. He was keeping her safe. My article hurt his reputation, but he let it go in order to protect his friend."

"He sounds like a true gentleman. What was it like living with Liam for nearly three months?"

I touch my cheek and try to hide my goofy smile. "It was the best three months of my life. We argued. Kissed. And made up so many times—it was like we'd been married for years." I tuck my hands under my chin. "What started off as a fake marriage between enemies, turned into something truly wonderful. Liam Ashley has changed my perspective of men. Well-known professional players in particular. I had him pegged as a man without integrity."

Alicia leans forward. "So, where does this reporting scandal leave you and Liam now? Have you had a chance to discuss the situation?"

"That's why I'm here. First to clear Liam's name..." I turn and look intently into the camera lens. "And the second is to say to you, Liam Ashley, that I've learned the hard way. Lesson number three. You can be wrong about someone or something and it's okay to admit you're wrong. I'm sorry." I steady my voice to keep the raw emotion out. "I loved every minute of being married to you. And I will always love you, Liam." A lump forms in my throat. If I say anymore mushy mooch on national news, I'm going to end up in a heap of tears. I face Alicia and offer a small smile.

Alicia nods, her voice laced with empathy. "Wow. It sounds like you've been on quite the journey. Is there anything else you'd like to share with our viewers?"

I take a deep breath, and my heart expands with gratitude for this opportunity to make amends. "I want to express my sincerest apologies to Liam and to everyone who was affected by the misleading articles. I've learned the importance of journalistic integrity and the power our words hold. Moving forward, I'm committed to transparency and responsible reporting, ensuring that the truth always shines through."

As the camera switches off, a sense of relief comes over me. I've taken a step toward rebuilding trust with Liam. If he will accept my apology, that is.

A man in beige business pants and a buttoned-down shirt approaches us with determined strides.

Alicia touches my arm. "Oh, that's Daryl, coming our way."

I swipe moisture from under my eyes and rise to my feet.

Daryl cups my hand and shakes enthusiastically. "A pleasure to meet the famous Trina Smith. I'm a big fan of the show."

Alicia gives us a formal introduction and we take our seats at the picnic table. Daryl gestures to the camera guy. "Show me the interview. Let's make sure we've got everything we need."

Daryl studies the playback screen, smiling and nodding along. "Love this. It's perfect."

He turns to me, and the creases around his eyes relax. "I like the way you handled the situation, Trina. You've explained that you were out of communication with the newspaper, so they ran with the article, reflecting your strained relationship." He touches my hand. "But you know they've used you, right? They tainted your reputation right along with Liam's." He shakes his head. "You're not going to keep working for them, are you?"

I nibble on a fingernail. He's right. The last article makes Trina Smith look like a heartless cow. My journal videos were accurate. I shared my feelings about Liam and my struggle with falling in love with him. It was all true.

"No. I won't be working for them anymore." Mike wouldn't have me back anyway, and I'm furious at how he let those exaggerated articles go to print without a word to me.

"Fantastic news, because I have an offer for you." Daryl's grin widens.

I gape at him. "You do?"

He squeezes my hand and lets go. "You have a great personality for TV. I've been watching the show. I admit, my wife and I are totally addicted. We've been voting for you and Liam. When I found out you're a sports journalist, my mind went racing. You'd be perfect for our sports news department. Live interviews at the games. Same as you've been doing, but in front of the cameras and triple the paycheck."

I gasp and slap a hand over my mouth. "Seriously? You're offering me a job at CNN?" This is the pinnacle of sports journalism elitism.

"Sure am. What do you say?" He spreads his arms.

I hug Daryl's neck. "Yes!"

We laugh together, and Alicia and the cameraman join in.

I pull back and touch my cheeks. "I can't believe this is happening. Thank you, Daryl. This is wonderful news." My smile fades. "Good news for my career, despite my marriage falling apart on national TV."

He pats my hand. "It's not over yet. How are you going to get Liam to watch tonight's broadcast?"

I sit up taller. "You're going to air it tonight?"

"For sure."

I nod slowly. "I know exactly who to call to make sure he's watching."

Chapter 19

I've never had a worse practice in my life. I missed over a dozen shots, and my running times were absolute garbage. All because of Trina. I groan and drop onto the bleachers.

Tandy races past, dribbling the ball like there's no tomorrow. The only time the man has any rhythm is on the court. He whistles and shoots the ball toward the net. It swooshes in and he jogs backward, shooting air pistols.

Cool drops onto the bench beside me and wraps a towel around his neck. He doesn't say anything. None of them do. They've treated today's practice like any other.

I could hug every last one of them. Sadly, not talking has made it all worse.

Coach comes out of his office and blows his whistle, motioning for us to join him.

Grabbing a towel, I shuffle along behind my teammates.

Coach meets my eyes, and I swear his anger and sadness combine before reaching out to zap me. He scans the team and chomps on his gum. "Meeting tonight at six. I want you all there. We need all hands on deck to figure out a strategy for dealing with the press. Liam's reputation is on the line."

He doesn't say *again,* but I cringe anyway. Why do these things keep happening to me? I'm sick of it.

"I expect all of you to bring it in. You're a team, and you will act like it on and off the court." Coach angles a finger at each of us in turn. "Right?"

"Yes, sir," we all call back in unison.

I run the towel over my face and neck. I can't wait to hop in the shower. Normally I'd be anxious to get home and see Trina. What do I have waiting for me now? I can't face that empty house. Even worse would be going home and finding Trina still there.

Cool slings his long arm over my shoulders and rocks me back and forth. "Chin up, man. We got this."

I dredge up a smile and jab a fist into his ribs. "I'll remember that next time you're heartbroken."

Cool leans away from me and takes his time scouring my face. He whistles. "You were really into this one. I thought it was all part of the show. When you came down this morning, you were too mad for me to see the truth." He ruffles my hair. "Sorry it came to this." He pauses. "You sure she's that bad? No chance it was a mistake?"

I shake my head and pull away. "Nah. She meant to ruin me. It's a good thing I found out now instead of later. Before I fell any harder."

"Don't think there *is* any harder than where you are right now." Cool points straight at me, his finger so close I almost go cross-eyed. "You love her. Like the real kind of love."

"Glad it took you so long to notice. I might have a prayer of getting over her." I hurry into the locker room and to a minute of peace in the shower.

Not quiet, but peace. The showers are a riot of noise as the guys sing to whatever is on the speakers.

The sound of James crooning the newest Taylor Swift in falsetto is enough to make me laugh through the pain. Man. Cool's right. I got it bad.

I hurry out of the locker room and go straight to Coach's office. We've been practicing all day, and it's close enough to six I don't bother leaving the gym. I'll grab food on my way home...if I can convince my stomach to stop somersaulting long enough to eat.

Coach's office has been transformed into a meeting room. Chairs sit in two rows, enough for the whole team. His desk is pushed back against the wall, and he stands with his arms crossed.

"Coach," I say as I enter. "I'm sorry."

He puts his hands on his hips. "It's not your fault, Liam. We all pushed for you to accept the spot on the show. I should have realized the potential fallout should anything go badly. We wanted publicity."

"But not this kind," I finish for him.

It was a gamble going on the show. I expected it to be complicated, but I never dreamed I'd fall in love with Trina of all people, only to have it backfire on me. Again.

Jeez, I'm a broken record. Love for me is like a bad shot at the hoop. The ball smashes against the glass and rebounds, then it's a free for all.

He rubs his neck and motions for me to take a seat. "Let's take it one day at a time. Things in this industry are never static. And reality TV is no different. In a few days, another sensational story will make headlines, and you'll be off the hook. In the meantime, we just have to figure out how to keep you safe."

I hear the others coming our way, their steps loud now that we're practicing.

Cool enters first, followed by Tandy. They take a seat, one on either side of me, showing their solidarity. The rest of the players file in and fill the chairs. Thank goodness we all showered. I can't imagine the stench if we'd all piled in this tiny room after practice. Even my socks dripped sweat when I peeled them off.

"Alright." Coach slaps his hands together and puts his fingers under his chin. He waits for the room to quiet, which doesn't take long. "What's our first step?"

"Beat the stuffing out of the Morgans tomorrow night and make everyone forget about Liam's problems?" offers someone in the back.

Coach grins. "Aside from that?"

Cool stands. "We should find out exactly what's being said." He looms over Coach, his expression sincere. "We don't know what we're up against if we're sitting here in the dark."

He's right, but the last thing I want is to hear what they're saying about me.

Cool taps the button on the TV. The screen flickers and fades in and out of focus for several seconds.

The guys groan. "Coach, when you gonna get a new TV? That thing's a relic."

Coach grins.

The picture stabilizes, and I suck in a sharp breath. Trina sits at a picnic table with a woman who's holding a CNN microphone. They look like old friends, and the sight churns my gut. I don't want to see her. "Turn it off." I lock my teeth and growl when Cool turns up the volume.

My ears ring, and all I see is Trina. As much as I want to hate her, my pulse still slams hard against my ribs. I wish I still had the right to kiss her. Good grief, I'm pathetic. She was right. I'm nothing but a love-sick pup.

I'm about to stand and leave the room when a single sentence cuts through the anger wrapping me so tight I didn't hear anything she said before.

"I will always love you, Liam." The sweetest words in the world come from Trina's lips.

The world stops turning. I can't breathe. Can't move. Can't think.

Is this for real? It can't be. How can I possibly believe she meant it?

"Play it back, Cool." Coach sits on the corner of his desk, arms crossed and a tiny smile on his lips.

Cool grabs the remote. "Man, I love technology."

He backs up the interview to the beginning. I watch Trina's face, searching desperately for any sign of sincerity.

Emotions play out in slow motion. Her eyes are red, her face slightly blotchy. Has she been crying? Is it terrible to hope she was? Because that's all I've wanted to do all day, bawl over what I lost.

She says the article wasn't hers. That she didn't approve it. I glance at Coach, whose head lowers in the smallest nod. He said he knew Trina's boss from before.

When we reach the end for the second time, Cool pauses the screen. He's caught Trina in a moment where she appears completely vulnerable and open, an instant after she admitted she loves me.

What am I supposed to believe?

"I spoke to Mike, Trina's boss, a few minutes ago. He confirms her story." Coach speaks slowly, like he knows I'm having trouble making up my mind and processing this whole dumpster-fire of a day.

"What about that?" I point at the TV. "Look. She said she loves me. How am I supposed to believe that?" Even as I say it, I feel myself softening toward her. Her boss used her like I thought she'd used me.

We both left this reality show with some new emotional scars.

Cool shifts his weight and crosses his arms. "Yeah, Liam." He points the remote at the TV and replays the last sentence again. "Look at that." He stops and catches my eye. "I'm no expert, but I'd say the woman is head over heels, totally in love with you."

"What you gonna do about it?" Tandy asks. He slaps a hand to my shoulder.

"One more thing." Coach interrupts. "Trina no longer works for Mike. He calls the parting amicable, but I'm doubting it's true. However, I have it on good authority Trina accepted a position with CNN as their new live-on-site reporter. Which means she'll be at the game tomorrow night."

My stomach and heart drop to the floor, leaving me feeling gutted. How am I supposed to play with her right there, within my sight the whole time?

If today's practice is any indication, Coach might as well bench me now.

"I've an idea." Tandy slaps my shoulder again. "You'll love this. Trina will too."

He fills us all in on his brilliant plan. I have to admit it's ingenious. But is it what I want? Once I make this move, there's no going back.

"Liam." Coach motions for me to follow him.

While the rest of the team rattles on about tomorrow night, Coach pulls me into the corner where the bleachers and the wall meet.

"What's wrong?" My stomach knots. Will he ask me to leave the team?

Coach gestures toward the doors tucked at the back of the gym. "There's someone here to meet you."

"Coach, I don't think I should be doing interviews right now." I rub a hand over my head and shrug an apology.

"It's not an interview." He grimaces. "I'm not that mean to you guys." He drags me away from the office. "I think you should hear what he has to say. You need to know all your options."

I'm about to argue when he shoves open the door leading to the lobby and I see Tony Preston—the owner of the Blue Jackals, the US's number one basketball team—standing there in his iconic blue suit.

My mouth drops open.

Coach nods. "Tony." He sounds congenial enough, but there's an undercurrent of tension in his voice and the way he shakes the other coach's hand. Coach pats my shoulder. "Come see me when you're done here."

"Well now." Tony thrusts a hand in my direction. "Liam Ashley. You're having quite the day."

"Week. Month. Months." I try to blow off the feeling of inferiority and shake the man's hand. "This whole thing has been a comedy of errors."

"All but one thing." Tony holds up a finger. "Seeing you on that show had me taking another look at your time on the court." He grins and gives a short whistle. "You know, I almost made a move on you three years ago, but I didn't."

"Why?" The question is rude, but I'm kind of over being worried about what one person thinks. I've hundreds of thousands of people watching my day to day life and commenting on every aspect of it. I'm over it.

Tony tilts his head and sizes me up like he's never seen me before. "Because I thought you were a B string player. I hoped you'd prove me wrong, and you did. This has been your best year to date, and I don't see that momentum slowing anytime soon."

Hope slips into the cracks made by Trina's betrayal. Wait. I correct myself. What I perceived as her betrayal.

"Sir, I need you to be real straight with me right now. Are you offering me a spot on your team?" I sound incredulous. Heck, I *feel* incredulous. No doubt it's plastered all over my face.

Tony's smile is as iconic as his suit, and when he allows it now, I can't help taking a step back. His laughter follows me. "Come on, son. You don't think I'd fly all the way here from California just to say hello, do you?"

I don't know. Seriously. I know nothing about the guy except what I've heard. Most of which is good. He has the number one ranking team, so he must be good. His attitude here is pleasant, even if a bit snotty. I can overlook that.

"We'll be compensating you with a house and car, all moving expenses paid by us. You'll also be put on the A string, first ones out on the court. Keep showing me the skill I've been seeing here, and we'll both be very happy people." He taps his finger to his chin. "Oh, and we'll be doubling your current salary, with room for that to grow."

Depending on how I play. That part is never said, but every ballplayer knows if they start tanking, their salary gets cut. Part of the business of being an athlete. Which is why most guys get into commercials and sponsored products.

I have never been more at a loss for words. I open my mouth. Close it. Open it again. Nothing comes out.

I'm torn by two futures. In one hand, I have the chance to make things right with Trina. In the other, I hold the power over my career and my future. More money than I ever imagined.

For a kid who grew up with nothing, money is a powerful motivator. I'd be lying to myself if I didn't admit I'm intrigued by more money, a bigger house, and a better car.

And I'd be leaving all this behind.

No more worries about Trina and what the reality show would demand of me next.

No deals for more shows in the future. I'd be sure to add that clause into my new contract with Tony.

There's a third option: take the job and ask Trina to move with me.

I'd be a jerk to ask that of her after she landed a spot with CNN. Unless they could find her a spot in California. Surely they could.

I could have it all. The money, the fame, and the wife.

Chapter 20

Tony stares me down. He doesn't say anything, but his eyes tighten when I don't immediately jump at his offer. Sorry, pal. I've learned my lesson. "I need some time to think it over."

He nods, though he looks unhappy. "Sure, sure." He whips out a business card and hands it over. "My assistant's number is on there. You give us a call when you decide."

Is he implying I'll come running the minute he walks away?

I'll admit, it's tempting. With every step of his polished shoes, a tiny portion of that future slipping away. Am I making a terrible mistake by not jumping on his offer?

I can't think straight. Too much has happened. I tap the card against my palm, then slide it into my shorts pocket. The door bangs shut behind Tony, and I stand immobile as he climbs into a cherry red convertible and peels out of the parking lot.

I grin as the image reminds me of Cool's fancy moves this morning, and there's a sudden catch in my throat. My team is here. These guys have had my back since day one. Could I walk away from that?

All I know about the Blue Jackals is that they're fierce on the court. I've seen them play, and we've played against them in the past.

When they're on the court, they're incredible. A memory resurfaces. They stood together off the court at a press conference last year. None of them looked at each other. It was like they were complete strangers.

Not what I want. I like the companionship and camaraderie here. I enjoy my life here. Sure the extra money would be awesome. I'd send it to my parents even though they swear they don't need it.

The gym door bursts open and Cool strides out. His eyes narrow. "You okay?"

"Yeah, man. I'm good." It's the truth, and for the first time all day, I feel like smiling. "Let's figure out this whole mess about tomorrow night."

"Got you covered." Cool pushes me ahead of him and keeps pushing until I'm across the court and back in Coach's office.

His gaze finds mine, and worry slips past his calm expression.

I shake my head *no*, hoping he understands.

A smile breaks out and he slaps his thighs. "Alright. I'm officially kicking the lot of you out of my office. Go plan this somewhere else." He shoos us out, flapping his hands and pushing Tandy when the guy's too slow to leave his chair.

I nod an I'll-be-right-behind-you to the others and stay behind.

Coach waits until Cool closes the door to speak. "You're saying *no* to Tony Preston?" He says it like he can't believe it.

Honestly, I don't blame him. I'm having trouble believing it. "I belong here. You brought me onto this team. You and those guys out there are the reason Tony wants me." I shake my head. "I'm not leaving."

Coach laughs. "I'm happy to hear that. Real happy." He braces his hands on the desk and shoves it back to its usual spot. "Now get out there and figure out this Trina issue."

"The Trina issue," as it turns out, has been turned over to Cool and Tandy. The two of them sit huddled together on the lowest bleacher while the other guys dribble balls and pass them to each other.

"Oh, do that again." Cool bites the pencil he's holding. "Can you make a beat like this?" He drums on his thighs.

The guys shake their heads. "It'd be too loud to hear you."

James spins a ball around on his finger. "I'll talk to the sound guy. Tell me what song you need."

I don't know whether to stop them or roll with it. Cool must sense my indecision because he jumps to his feet. "You're not shutting this down. It's too late."

I throw up my hands in a show of surrender. "Sure. Fine. Do I even need to be here?"

"Yep." James throws the ball at me. "Food's on its way." He tosses my cell phone next. "And your brother called. He's bringing the food."

I roll my eyes. Leave it to my brother to finagle an invitation to join us for dinner. Not that he hasn't met the guys before. They treat him like he's *their* brother.

My phone rings as I snatch it from the air. Clay's name shows on the screen and I answer.

"Open the door for me," he says before I even say hello. "Hurry. The food's heavy."

I laugh and jog over to the door we all come and go from and unlock it for Clay. He staggers in, his arms filled with pizza boxes.

His phone slides from his ear and lands on top of the stack, but he doesn't seem to notice.

The guys swarm him, taking the pizzas. A few slap Clay on the back and shoulders until I'm sure his skin is red.

He grabs my arm before I can follow the guys. "Are you okay?"

I get him up to speed on what's happened from the articles to Tony's offer.

His eyes widen. "You need to call Mom. Tell her what you just told me. She's madder than a wet cat." Another of Grandpa's favorite expressions. Great. Clay and I are both starting to sound like the old man.

I should have called her before now, but things had been so crazy I forgot. "I'll do it now."

Clay hurries away, and the team greets him with cheers and whistles. My brother, the pediatric surgeon and hero of my teammates' hearts. He brings them food, and they love him for his humor and jokes. And no wonder, he's a great guy. I couldn't have a better brother.

The landline rings and rings. Mom and Dad's cellphones are dead half the time, so I always call the house phone.

Finally, Mom answers. "Sorry, Liam. I had to make sure it wasn't another of those reporters." She huffs. "They've been calling here all day. Your dad hung up on one not ten minutes ago."

"I told you not to answer unknown callers, especially when the media's eating me alive." I sigh and pinch the bridge of my nose. "Listen, everything is a madhouse right now, but it'll settle down, okay? Ignore the phone unless it's family. Are you and Dad coming to the game? I'll have security waiting for you."

"Wouldn't miss it," Dad bellows from somewhere in the background. "What're you gonna do about your wife?"

"You'll find out at the game." The guys call for me to hurry up. "Trust me, it's all good." I tell them what I can about Trina and end with a promise. "See you tomorrow."

I make another call before joining my team. Tony's assistant answers with a tone that borders on surly. I make my point in quick, concise words, thanking them for the opportunity but ultimately rejecting the offer.

There's a moment of shocked silence before I hang up.

Now to get ready for tomorrow.

Trina is in for the surprise of her life. I hope she doesn't mind that I haven't called her yet. I want to. I spin the phone around in my hand and open her contact information. It would be so easy to call and apologize.

But I need a bigger apology. A sure-fire way to get her attention and ensure she listens to everything I need to say.

TRINA

After my interview with CNN that day, I returned to Liam's apartment and collected my belongings. I intended to bunker in a hotel for a couple of nights while waiting to see if Liam would call me, but Pam and Dalton begged me to stay with them. It's a bit of a commute from their place to the new office, but it's nice to be with family at a time like this.

I place my dinner plate into the dishwasher in slow motion like the plate weighs a brick.

The aroma of garlic, basil, and a hundred other seasonings linger in the air. Unfortunately, I only pecked at my dinner and couldn't finish dessert. Not after my interview aired, and Liam not calling the second it finished. Coach promised me he'd have the whole team watching.

The overhead chandelier bathes the kitchen in light. White cabinets and gold-burnished handles sparkle. The marble countertops are a rich mottled gray with flecks of emerald. Dalton and Pam's place is simply gorgeous.

Pam enters the kitchen. Her face is pinched and her lips pursed. She shoes me out of the kitchen. "No need to be in here. James is still around. He'll finish cleaning up for the night."

I scan the brilliant stainless-steel appliances. The kitchen already looks spotless. Oh, how my sister's life changed when she married a billionaire. They have their own personal chef. James cooked an amazing three-course meal. I hope James puts the crème me brulée in the fridge. I might need a midnight snack when I can't sleep. I'll have to build a pillow wall around me so it feels like home. No. Liam's apartment wasn't home. His unbroken silence proves he hasn't forgiven me. But instead of being consigned to the couch, I'm here, staying in a three-story mansion.

My rambunctious nephew barrels into the kitchen like a pint-sized hurricane. I laugh. His silly escapades are the perfect distraction from my melancholy mood. Time to be the fun auntie. Melanie would slap me silly if I said that out loud. We have this unspoken competition going on for the role of favorite auntie. I'm easily the winner since I see Rex more often. Melanie moved to Washington State.

I chase after him, and he shoots up the spiral staircase. My arms flail like a clumsy penguin trying to catch a slippery fish. The kid is fast.

"Rex, slow down, buddy." I gasp for breath when I reach the top step. "Where are you?" I scan the hall left and right.

He giggles mischievously, his laughter filling the hall like a chorus of tiny hyenas.

Agh. He's hiding behind the door to the study.

I crouch and extend my arms while holding my breath. Tiptoeing toward the door, I wince each time the floorboards creak.

But Rex must sense my every move. He zigzags from his hiding spot and into the study with the agility of a mini ninja.

"You can't escape me! I've trained with athletes, and I'm a force to be reckoned with."

Rex pokes his head around the corner and sticks his tongue out.

What? The little rascal. What would Super Nanny do? He can't get away with that.

I launch into the study, ready to tell Rex that making such faces is unacceptable.

But there stands Dalton, and he looks grumpy.

I stop in my tracks, stunned. Rex is completely captivated by Dalton. And still for once. Does the man have some secret superpower over children?

I clear my throat. "Um, Dalton, sorry to barge in like that. I didn't know you were up here."

Dalton's eyes meet mine. His expression is unyielding. "Apparently, so."

He raises an eyebrow, but his serious demeanor cracks, and a smile breaks free. "The kid knows I have a secret stash of cookies that only well-behaved children can access. That's why he's frozen for five seconds. But just watch. He won't be able to stay still any longer than that."

"Can too," Rex's lips don't move as he mumbles in his adorable voice.

Dalton starts counting down. "Five, four, three . . ."

Little Rex's knee wobbles. His arm twitches.

". . . two, one, zero."

Rex leaps into a star jump. "I did it. I lasted more than five seconds." He holds out his small palm. "Cookie, please."

I fold my arms across my chest. "Does Pam know about this secret stash?"

Simultaneously, Rex and Dalton hold a finger to their lips. "Shh."

I roll my eyes. "Fine." I hold out my hand as well. "I want one too."

My back pocket buzzes, and I jump a mile in the air. Cellphone. "It could be Liam."

I turn and race out of the study, slipping out the phone. My heart free falls when the screen flashes Melanie's name.

"What's up?" I say flatly.

"Has he called yet?" Her voice is filled with expectation.

"Nope. Not yet." I make my way down the hall and slip into the library.

I'm greeted by rows and rows of mahogany shelves filled with book spines. I might sleep in here tonight. The fireplace makes the place look inviting. I probably won't be able to sleep anyway.

"Don't worry. He'll call after a confession like that," Melanie says. "I didn't know you had it in you to be that sweet."

I slap my free hand to my forehead. "Yeah. I can't believe I said all that on the news. And tomorrow I need to report on his game."

"What?"

"My first day at CNN, and they're sending me to Liam's game. How strategic is that?"

"Oh, maybe that's why he hasn't called. He wants to talk to you in person after the game."

"You think so?"

"I bet that's it. Oh, Trina, you have nothing to worry about. That man loves you."

Warmth swirls in my belly. Melanie's right. The way Liam looks into my eyes and connects with my soul shows how much he loves me. I can't wait to tell him how I feel face to face tomorrow at the game. And if he doesn't forgive me, it's going to be super awkward interviewing him and his team.

Chapter 21

TRINA

I stand on the sidelines. The roar of the crowd envelopes me as Liam and his team dominate the basketball court. The familiar scent of sweat and anticipation hangs in the air, and the energy is palpable. It's been twenty-four hours since my public confession, and the tension between us weighs heavy in my heart.

Liam's team holds a comfortable lead. They've come back from a low score in the first quarter, and the scoreboard reflects their hard work and determination. I can't help my sense of pride as he plays with a fire in his eyes. His athletic skill is on full display, captivating the audience and reminding me of the man I fell in love with.

But what if he still holds a grudge? What if my public apology on national TV wasn't enough to mend the damage? Will he ever forgive me? Will he give us a chance to rebuild what was shattered?

I study Liam's every move, hoping to catch a glimpse of any foretelling emotion. His focus is unwavering. He's in his element, giving it his all on the court.

I scan the crowd for their responses. And that's when I spot him—Nicholas, the producer from "Bride at First Sight." He didn't seem the sporty type, but I could be wrong. Unless he's here to meet with Liam after the game. But why?

Nicholas waves and weaves his way through the bleachers, his eyes locked on mine. Apprehension flutters in my stomach as I brace for what he might say. As he reaches me, he offers a warm smile.

"Trina! You won't believe the craziness going on." Deep lines bracket his mouth. "The voting line for you and Liam has gone absolutely bonkers. The fans are demanding your return for the finale night."

My eyes widen, the implications of his words sinking in. Viewers have rallied behind us. Maybe my vulnerability won them over.

I touch my stomach. The thought of reuniting with Liam on the grand finale makes me giddy. If I held my microphone to my belly, it would start singing a nervous karaoke rendition of 'Don't Stop Believin'.

"But Nicholas . . ." My fingers pitter pat over my chest as I attempt to calm myself. "What if Liam doesn't want to return? Have you spoken to him? He hasn't said anything about wanting to stay married to me."

Nicholas leans in closer and lowers his voice, which makes it difficult to hear in an arena full of super fans. "Liam may not have said anything yet, but actions speak louder than words. I called his coach after your public apology, and he insisted I come tonight and speak with you both." He rubs his hands like it's a done deal and of course, Liam is fully on board with the idea.

Nicholas continues, a glint in his eyes, "I have a strong feeling that Liam might surprise you. He's not one to let go easily." He points to the court. "Look at the guy. Defying the rules of gravity."

Liam hangs on the ring after a slam dunk. That's my man.

I swallow hard. The viewers believe we can make this arranged marriage last. And I believe it too.

As Nicholas walks away, leaving me with hope that Liam and I could still become the winning couple for the show, I feel somewhat pumped.

The halftime buzzer blares. I steady myself for what comes next. Will Liam seek me out? Will he finally address the elephant in the room, or will he continue to keep his feelings locked away like I used to do?

LIAM

Energy pulses through my veins as the halftime buzzer sounds. Sweat drips down my forehead, and my heart races. We're ahead by three points. The game has been fierce, but nothing prepared me for seeing Trina on the sidelines. I almost approached her earlier, but Cool held me back.

He grabs my arm now and gives me the signal. It's time. Ours and the opposing team's cheerleaders already know what's up. They stand along the sidelines, waving their hands and encouraging the audience to clap with them.

The stadium erupts in cheers as our team takes center stage. Time to shine.

Tandy grabs the microphone. Cool, tonight's self-proclaimed beatboxer, positions himself on one side of the court, ready to unleash his rhythm. The crowd's roar subsides as Tandy speaks.

As Cool starts up in the background, I realize why he told James to forget about the guy in the sound room. In all our years as a team, I've never seen this side of Cool. It's impressive. Even better than his dancing at mine and Trina's wedding. From the corner of my eye, I sneak a peek in her direction to make sure she's watching.

None of this matters if she's not listening.

Tandy lifts a hand. "Ladies and gentlemen, boys and girls, welcome to the show. It's time to witness the flow. But first, let me introduce the man of the hour, our star player, Liam Ashley!"

The spotlight finds me, and I push the weight of the game aside and step forward. The court transforms into our personal playground as I take the microphone from Tandy, ready to unleash my emotions.

I take in a breath. This is for Trina. "Yo, yo, let's bring the heat. We're the champions, it's time to compete. We've come this far, we won't back down, we'll fight till the end, and take the crown."

The crowd's energy intensifies, feeding my adrenaline. My teammates join me, forming a tight-knit circle as we sway to the beat of Cool's contagious rhythm. The crowd follows suit, swaying in unison.

Cool's beatboxing creates the perfect stomping beat, and the crowd joins in. The entire stadium rumbles. They have no idea where I'm going, but they're in.

Cool or even Coach, must've talked to the other team. They drum along with Cool, and one of their guys jumps in with a beat of his own.

We might be competitors during the game, but right now, it's like we're family.

I search for Trina as Cool's beatboxing drops into the background.

This is it. "Now listen up, Trina, this one's for you. It's time to say the words I've been longing to. We've been through thick and thin, ups and downs, but I want you to know, I'm done messing around."

She wraps one arm around her waist. Her microphone dangles from the tips of her fingers. I hold her gaze, willing her to see me and understand that I'm sorry, and I want to make things right.

A second spotlight zooms in on Trina. She shields her eyes at first, then resumes hugging her middle.

Tandy runs up and down the court alongside my teammates. They dance to the beat. Several of them grab basketballs and run through a few of our more intricate practice drills, turning it into a dance.

The cheerleaders keep the crowd in rhythm. My message of love echoes throughout the stadium.

I pick up the next line, grateful Cool stayed late with me last night to make sure I had the words right. "Trina, I'm sorry for the times I let you down. But standing here today, I'm turning it around. Will you take my hand as my wife? I'll love you forever. Let's start our new life."

The lyrics hang in the air. My heart pounds until I think it might burst. The crowd falls silent, holding their breath, as if time itself has paused. Then, a smile creeps across Trina's face. Tears shimmer in her eyes.

She lifts the microphone to her lips, says something to the camera guy, then lowers the mic to her chair. Her smile widens, and she moves toward me.

The entire stadium takes a collective breath. This is the moment I've waited for all my life. I fell in love with Trina a long time ago.

Once she's right in front of me, I see the faintest shimmer of tears in her eyes. She takes my microphone and holds it under her chin. Her voice is steady, her eyes latched on mine like I'm the only person she sees. "Liam, you've always been the one for me. I'll gladly be your wife, for all eternity."

The crowd erupts into thunderous applause. Love does conquer all. It might not ensure we win this game, but as far as I'm concerned, I've won something infinitely better.

This moment will forever be etched in my memory.

We've won more than a basketball game. We've won love and the chance to build a future together. As the crowd roars, I know this halftime show has become the start of something beautiful.

I sweep her into my arms and kiss her for everyone to see. Let the cameras roll and come what may tomorrow. I care about this moment, right now, with the love of my life holding onto my face and kissing me with enough passion to make me spontaneously combust.

"I love you," I whisper against her lips.

Her arms wind around my neck and she squeezes tight. "I love you too."

"Hey, Lover Boy," Cool shouts at me, his beatboxing mission complete. "Back to the game."

The team whistles and cheers.

Mine and Trina's faces take up the entire megatron. I see myself smiling like a goof. "You'll marry me? In a real wedding. With messy lava cakes and Wrecking Ball Rex knocking the cake over?"

"And Granny Smith belching and hitting on your teammates." Trina laughs and pats my cheeks. "Yes, Liam."

I kiss her one last time before backing away. Forever looks pretty good from here.

Chapter 22

TRINA

All of the contestants stand backstage, huddled behind a black curtain. My heart pounds in my ears as I cling onto Liam's arm, ready to hit the stage for the finale night of "Bride at First Sight."

Liam leans down and places a kiss on my forehead. "It doesn't matter if we lose, babe. The show brought us together. We've won the prize already."

I squeeze his hand. "You're very sweet. But still, I want to win this." I point through the curtain. "Look, our families are on the front row."

Liam's parents and his brother, Clay, sit beside my family. Mom and Dad hold hands. Melanie and Pam sit with their spouses. And little Rex is wriggling on Gran's lap. That kid better not run on stage and take over the show. I wouldn't put it past him.

The show's host, Martin Cortez, swings his arms wide. "Let's bring on the remaining four couples. Please, welcome to the stage, Victor and Regina!"

Regina smacks Victor's bottom to get him moving, and he jumps through the gap of the curtain like an obedient circus monkey.

"Matt and Deborah!"

Deborah and her man are joined at the hip, not an inch of space between them as they slink onto the stage.

"William and Alyssa!"

Alyssa seems much more relaxed around William. They are competition for sure. She's so soft and sugary sweet. Which I am not.

Liam gives me a side hug. "We're next. Here goes."

"Liam and Trina!"

Hand in hand we move with confidence onto the stage. A force to be reckoned with. Bring it on.

Dazzling lights adorned the stage, and a giant screen displays the "Bride at First Sight" logo.

"Tonight, we'll find out who our viewers voted as the couple most likely to succeed in marriage. It's not too late to place your final vote."

On the bottom of the screen, the newlywed's names scroll in blue font. Four voting lines to choose from.

"We'll go through the highlights of each couple's journey over the past three months, starting with Victor and Regina."

Oh, boy. This will be good.

Hidden camera footage appears onto the screen. Regina stomps into the living room. She holds up a toilet roll to Victor, who's slouching on the sofa.

In an exasperated tone, she huffs. "The toilet paper should face forward, Victor."

Behind Victor, in the corner of the room, Regina's pet parrot squawks with impeccable timing. "Idiot. Idiot."

The audience bursts into laughter.

I slap a hand to my mouth. "Oh, man," I whisper to Liam. "What have they got on us?"

He squeezes my hand. "It's all good fun. Don't worry."

As the video montage continues, showcasing the ups and downs of each couple, my nervousness builds.

Soon enough, it's our turn. Pam points to the screen, and Rex sits still. Melanie links arms with Adam, sitting on the edge of her seat. Mom and Dad look a little worried. Granny Smith lets out a dog whistle.

I'm not embarrassed this time. I have an inkling my tenacious spirit comes from Gran. That'll be me in forty-years', embarrassing my grandkids.

The overhead screen shows the infamous moment when Liam slaps my sticky note "don't drink from the carton" to his own forehead and proceeds to guzzle half its contents. Little did he know, I was standing at the entrance to the dining area, hands on hips. When he turns and spots me, milk dribbles down his chin. The crowd erupts, and I can't help but join in the laughter, shaking my head at the memory.

The next scene shows me and Liam smooching in various corners of the apartment. Once in the walk-in pantry, another time over the kitchen countertop when I smothered chocolate over his mouth and had to kiss it off. Things got a bit hectic in the laundry room, and all the neatly folded clothes ended up crumpled on the floor. The couch, the couch, and the couch again. The sizzling kiss by the window before he scooped me up and headed for the bedroom. My cheeks do go hot at that one. And finally, the balcony where we watched a beautiful sunset together.

Liam hugs me from behind and kisses my neck. "Love you, wifey."

I secretly nudge him in the ribs. He knows I hate it when he calls me that.

Martin, the host, armed with his charismatic charm and a few well-timed jokes, keeps the audience engaged between the commercial breaks. His banter with us and the other couples adds a light-hearted touch to the tense atmosphere. He cracks a joke about Liam's infamous milk carton incident, making the entire room burst into laughter once again.

Finally, the moment arrives. Martin takes a deep breath. "And now, ladies and gentlemen, the votes are in. Let's find out which couple the viewers have chosen as the most likely to remain married and live happily ever after."

My heartbeat mimics the drumroll and the suspense builds. I hold my breath, stealing a quick glance at Liam, who looks just as nervous as I am. His eyebrows are furrowed, and he keeps fidgeting.

The host opens the envelope, and the corner of his eyes crinkle. "The couple who has captured the hearts of America, the couple deemed most likely to have a lifetime of wedded bliss, is none other than . . . Trina and Liam!"

A wave of relief and joy washes over me, and the room fills with cheers and applause. Liam and I exchange a stunned but elated look, our smiles widening with pure happiness. The journey may have been full of twists and turns, but somehow, we've won the hearts of America.

As we walk onto the stage toward Martin, hand and hand, streamers and confetti shower us from above. Flashing lights and whistles surround us. Our beautiful families stand and applaud, elated emotion clear on their faces.

Martin congratulates us both. Liam holds up our joined hands and the lyrics roll in my mind, "We are the champions."

Liam swirls me into a dance. He lowers me to the floor in a classic move and kisses me thoroughly. The crowd goes berserk.

When he raises me into a standing position, Nicholas appears from stage right with a massive corflute bank check. My eyes nearly pop out of my head at all the zeros. Sweet mercy. We're going on a real honeymoon . . . to Europe.

As I stand on that stage, hand in hand with Liam, the winner's check in front of us, a whirlwind of emotions leave me half-crying, half-laughing. Our journey on "Bride at First Sight" may have been filled with challenges, misunderstandings, and heated moments, but in the end, love prevailed. As I gaze into Liam's eyes, I know that we're ready to embrace this new chapter together. With a new trust as our foundation and an unwavering commitment to each other, we embark on our happily ever after. The cameras may have stopped rolling, but our love story has just begun.

WANT TO SEE MORE FROM the characters of *Love Unscripted*?

Read the first novel in the *Nantucket Romantic Comedies* series, *Amnesia on Nantucket.*

What happens when you wake up on your honeymoon and don't remember your husband?

When Melanie suffers an accident on her honeymoon and wakes up with amnesia, the last thing she expects is to find a hunky man in her bed. A man who swears is her husband, but she's not buying it. Armed with pepper spray and a kitchen knife, Melanie sets out across Nantucket, escaping her imposter husband and trying to find her way home.

Adam has no idea what he's going to do. He can't leave Melanie to wander alone, and even if she doesn't remember that she loves him, he promises to stand by her side. Through a series of hilarious mishaps and amnesia-induced adventures, Melanie and Adam stumble their way toward falling in love . . . for the second time. Maybe this time, Melanie won't forget.

Find this book and other Nantucket sweet romances at TarynDanielsAuthor.Wordpress.com

About the Author

TARYN DANIELS WRITES sweet romance on the shores of Nantucket. Aside from homeschooling and tending to her fluffy fur babies, Taryn spends every spare moment dreaming up awkward situations or swoony moments to entertain her readers.

Find out more at TarynDanielsAuthor.Wordpress.com

www.ingramcontent.com/pod-product-compliance
Lightning Source LLC
Chambersburg PA
CBHW030635120726
47904CB00006B/2159